The Coded Papyrus

A thrilling Egyptian adventure.

Enigma in Rome

Save Caesar and face Rome's hidden challenges.

The Cursed Empress

Navigate Atlantis's secrets to break a powerful curse.

The Sun Disk

Race against time to save the Incas.

The Magic Chalice

Spooky thrills in Dracula's realm.

The Great Christmas Rescue

An adventure into Santa's realm to save Christmas.

The Druids' Secret

A magical quest to recover Excalibur and reshape history.

Edited by Anna Bowles.
Proofread by Michele Chiappetta from Two Birds Author Services
(twobirdsauthorservices.com)
Cover art by Draftss (https://draftss.com/)

APICEM PUBLISHING

Apicem Publishing
1309 Coffeen Avenue STE 1200
Sheridan, WY 82801, United States
www.apicempublishing.com

Published in 2024
Text Copyright © Coline Monsarrat , 2023
Aria & Liam ® is a trademark of Coline Monsarrat, 2022
All rights reserved.

ISBN (paperback): 78-1-959814-15-3
ISBN (ebook): 978-1-959814-16-0

ARIA & LIAM
The History Detectives

THE DRUIDS' SECRET

Coline Montsarrat

APICEM PUBLISHING

Hey fellow adventurers, meet Liam! He is my best friend and partner in crime! He's a 13-year-old kid from Sommetville who can code up a storm and kick a soccer ball like a pro. When we're not in class, you can usually find him doing one of those things. Unless, of course, I've got some wild idea to drag us into trouble - and let's be honest, I usually do!

One time, I even dragged us straight into a 3,000-year-old kingdom. Can you believe it? At first, Liam wasn't exactly thrilled, especially when I started rambling on about history like a super-enthusiastic professor. Hey, I could talk about historical stuff for hours – it's my thing! But guess what? My nerdy history knowledge actually came in handy and saved our bacon more than a few times. And let's not forget Liam's mad archery skills – we'd be royally stuck without them!

Now we're like heroes of the past, with people from all over calling on us to save the day. It's pretty crazy, and even though Liam freaks out every time we get transported to a different time period, he secretly loves our adventures. Just don't tell him I said that, or he'll never let me live it down!

Hey there, fellow adventurers! Let me introduce you to my partner-in-crime, Aria! She's not your average 13-year-old - this girl has a serious obsession with history. Seriously, don't even try to challenge her, or she'll beat you every time. That's why I call her the walking encyclopedia!

Aria's motto is to live life to the fullest, even if it means breaking a few rules (which happens a lot when I'm around). But her curiosity is what led us on an epic adventure through the Kingdom of Ramesses II, a place that's older than my grandpa's grandpa's grandpa. At first, I wasn't too thrilled, but I have to admit, it's kind of grown on me (don't tell Aria, though!).

And get this, not only do we travel through time, but I also get to enjoy beating Aria in sports! I mean, who doesn't love the feeling of outsmarting your best friend?

So buckle up, adventurers, because Aria and I are about to take you on a wild ride through history!

CONTENTS

CONTENTS

THE DRUIDS' SECRET

Let the adventure begin

THE CHARACTERS

ARIA

LIAM

MERLIN

ARTHUR

TANGLEWOOD

FAEWIND

LANCELOT

CHAPTER I
THE SPORTAPALOOZA TOURNAMENT

The sun is slowly creeping over the horizon as Aria and Liam walk to Sommetville Junior High School. The autumn leaves cover the streets, providing a colorful setting for their journey to school. Sleepy Liam has his eyes half-closed, but Aria is full of energy, skipping along beside him.

"Aria, can you please calm down?! You're jumping like a kangaroo, and it makes me dizzy!" Liam exclaims, pressing a hand to his forehead.

"I'm warming up, my dear Liam!" Aria retorts cheerfully as she keeps hopping and flapping her arms around. "So should you if you want to win today!"

Liam rolls his eyes and hurries to catch up with

her. If she doesn't make history, her boundless energy will. Suddenly, their beloved dog, Pingo, rushes forward to meet Aria.

"Come on, Pingo, let's show Liam what mornings are for!" Aria shouts. "One, two, three…" she mutters as she executes a clumsy *pas de bourrée*.

Liam halts abruptly and turns round to give her a stern look. "Can you please just walk like a normal person? You'll hurt yourself again, and then I'll lose the tournament!"

Aria clenches her teeth as she slows down. She has to keep calm. This is the moment they've both been waiting for. Taking place every fall, the one-day Sportapalooza Tournament is the most anticipated sports event at Sommetville Junior High. Teams of two students go head-to-head in a series of three different sports. But here's the catch—until the day of the tournament, no one knows which contests they will be playing in.

Every year, Aria and Liam compete together. Despite Liam's grumbles about Aria's clumsiness and her criticism of his lack of strategy, they can't be separated. They know that they make an unbeatable team. And what could be better than winning a prize with your best friend?

"Okay, I'll calm down," Aria concedes. "But

please warm up! I don't want to see you sleeping on the field!"

"With you screaming, that's unlikely!" Liam retorts before adding, "Anyway, I don't see how we could lose. We are definitely the best!"

Aria grins widely. "My dear Liam, I could not agree more!"

"What sports do you think we'll have?" Liam muses, his eyes brightening with anticipation. "Basketball, for sure! That's definitely my specialty!" he adds before noticing Aria's confused expression. "Oh, I forgot basketball isn't really a good idea for you!"

"It's not that I'm a bad player. It's just that the hoop is too high for me!"

"Sure, spin the tale you fancy!" Liam laughs.

"You'd better not make fun of me," Aria warns, her eyes widening as she stares him down. "Because let me remind you that the CogniQuest Festival is coming soon, and you'll need me more than I need you!"

Liam pauses for a second; he knows that when it comes to history, he's no match for Aria—the walking encyclopedia, as he often calls her.

"Let's hope there's frisbee or..." Liam reconsiders.

"Dodgeball!" Aria suggests with a wide grin. "We probably should have practiced a bit! I heard Amelia and John have been training all summer."

"Nonsense, my dear Aria! We win every year!" Liam smirks.

Aria grins proudly. She and Liam have easily become the best team Sommetville Junior High School has ever seen. Without much effort on top of that!

They walk along in contented silence, thinking of the prize they'll win. A dreamy weekend in the most amazing amusement park ever, Sommetville SkyRide. They can already picture the wind blowing through their hair as they whizz around the Inferno SkySwirl, the most thrilling ride on Earth. Their tastebuds tingle at the thought of ChocoBerry Clouds, a famous traditional dessert in Sommetville —a heavenly combination of strawberry and choco-late blended into one magical cotton candy.

As they reach the school gates, their daydreaming comes to an abrupt end. Pingo sprints toward his two furry friends, Pippa and Suzy, who are waiting patiently with their owners.

"Finally, you made it!" Amelia exclaims.

"For a moment, we thought you must have cold feet!" Alex teases.

"Us? Cold feet?" Liam protests. "Prepare yourself for a thrashing!"

"Liam is correct! The winning duo has arrived!" Aria whoops as they head toward the cafeteria, eager to begin the tournament.

The sports field at the back of Sommetville Junior High School is buzzing as hundreds of students, faculty, and parents gather in the grandstands to watch the Sportapalooza tournament. The participants are waiting inside, trying to contain their excitement.

The bets are in, and the anticipation is at a fever pitch. Some people say there will be a rollerblade race, while others claim to have seen a skating rink set up near the lake. Liam has an air of confidence as he hops and stretches, making sure his body is ready. His expression turns serious when he looks at Aria, swinging her leg frantically from right to left.

"What is it?" she asks, noticing her friend's odd expression. "I'm warming up!"

"If you say so..." Liam responds sarcastically. "It looks more like a very bad circus routine, but you do what you want..."

The hall becomes still as the principal's words reach the ears of the audience. The contestants' excitement is palpable as the opening game approaches. Aria starts to jump around with her fists tightly clenched, barely containing her enthusiasm.

A TRUMPET SOUNDS, causing a flurry of excitement among the students. The refectory door swings open, and the students pour onto the competition grounds to be greeted by loud applause. Pingo and his furry pals bark loudly in encouragement, making a few people cover their ears.

"Look! Pingo's over there with your sister!" Aria exclaims.

Liam stares at her, eyes wide. "It's not like I can miss him—he barks as loud as his owner!" Liam retorts.

Aria is about to respond when Mrs. Montclair, the principal, signals from the podium for everyone to quiet down. The orchestra stops playing.

She speaks with a loud, clear voice. "Students! Welcome to the 100th Sportapalooza tournament!" The students erupt in chatter and cheers. "This year, you will have three exciting events—starting with…" She pauses for dramatic effect, making the crowd whisper in anticipation. "…Ice Gliders!"

Liam looks surprised, as he hadn't anticipated

this sport due to the warm weather. Aria grits her teeth, knowing her clumsiness will be a disadvantage.

"Followed by BranchBounceFlyers," the principal continues, which brings clapping and cheers from the audience. "And Frisbee!"

"Yes!" Aria and Liam shout in unison.

"Remember, the victorious team will be rewarded with a luxurious weekend at Sommetville SkyRide Park." Mrs. Montclair's announcement increases everyone's enthusiasm. "Let the competition begin! May the best team come out on top!" she proclaims to immense applause.

The students hurry to the assignment board to find out who they will be up against.

"Frisbee, Liam!" Aria cries.

"You're playing me and Amelia this time." John grins after looking at the board, eager to prove himself.

"I hope you've warmed up, because we're ready," Liam warns, high-fiving Aria.

Aria, Liam, John, and Amelia race toward the field where the competition will take place. Mr. Thornton, their physical education teacher, stands ready with the Frisbee firmly in his grasp.

The game is simple: each team consists of two

people who try to pass the Frisbee back and forth without it being intercepted by the opposition. Aria and John stand on one side of the field, with Amelia and Liam facing them. All four of them are jumping from foot to foot in anticipation as they prepare to catch the Frisbee. Getting a hold of it right at the beginning is important; they only have fifteen minutes to rack up as many points as they can, with each successful catch earning them one point.

"Are you ready for this?" Mr. Thornton asks, smiling as he tosses the Frisbee into the air. The players' eyes are fixed on the whirling disc above them. Suddenly, it begins its descent to the ground, and they take off in every direction, trying to antici-pate where it will come down.

As Aria jumps to catch the Frisbee, John runs past her and snatches it in mid-air.

"ARIA!" Liam scowls as he races ahead of Amelia before lunging for the flying disc, but he's too late.

"You're no better than me!" Aria yells, her voice trembling.

Amelia sprints around Liam to throw the Frisbee to her teammate. Realizing Aria is too short to jump up and catch it, Liam lunges for it. The Frisbee gradually slows down mid-air and turns toward the trees along the side of the field.

Aria and Liam charge ahead. They shout, "I got it!" in unison—then collide in mid-air. They both cry out in pain and fall flat on the ground, Aria on her back and Liam on his front.

Aria struggles to sit up, her back aching from the aftershock. Liam gently rubs his head, which is throbbing from the impact. Then they gape around in shock.

The cheers of the audience have been replaced by pure silence. Instead of the school field, they find themselves surrounded by a forest with trees so tall they seem to touch the sky. An ethereal fog clings to the ground.

They are no longer in Sommetville.

CHAPTER 2
MEETING WITH MERLIN

T he light fog shrouding the damp forest floor caresses Aria's and Liam's legs as they look around. Still half-stunned from the collision, Liam takes his time standing up. His labored breathing echoes through the woods, along with the crackling of leaves moving in the wind and squirrels munching on nuts.

He looks around in confusion, mumbling, "Where did we end up this time?"

"I'm guessing a forest," Aria replies as Liam rolls his eyes at her.

"You are a genius, my dear Aria!" he exclaims, raising his arm.

Aria swiftly stands up, her legs completely

covered in mud. "You ask a question, I answer, my dear Liam!" she retorts.

They stop arguing when they hear a shout in the distance. Through the foliage, they make out a figure running toward them. The thud of boots on leaves and twigs grows louder as he approaches. Now, they can clearly see a tall teenager wearing a wool tunic tucked into brown pants. His cloak, secured around his waist by a brooch, is brown too and flutters lightly behind him as he runs. His eyes widen as he approaches.

"Merlin! I found them!" he shouts, reducing his speed as he reaches the adventurers, who stand and stare at him. "You two must be Aria and Liam," the boy declares.

An elderly man emerges from the shadows. His white hair cascades down his torso, and a thick beard conceals the lower half of his wrinkled face. He is carrying a wooden staff and stumbles slightly as he nears them. "It worked!" he shouts with delight, nearly tripping over a tree root.

"Are you sure they're the right ones?" the boy asks, frowning as he stares at Aria and Liam.

The old man studies them for a few moments, head cocked to one side, before slowly replying, "I suppose so. I'm certain I cast the spell correctly. So, they must be!"

"I'm not trying to be cruel, Merlin," the boy clarifies as he faces the elderly man, "but your incantations haven't been working too well recently!"

"Merlin?" Aria stammers, coming out of her stupor.

"Like Merlin the druid?" Liam asks.

The old man's face lights up as he hears his name. "Do you know me?" he asks.

"Well, I wouldn't go so far as to say I know you… but I've definitely heard about you," Aria responds.

"And me, do you know me?" the teenage boy asks, puffing out his chest with a big smile.

The adventurers are amused as they take in the haughty figure before them. How can they tell him that they have no idea who he is? Eventually, Merlin breaks the silence with a sigh. "This is why we had to call for reinforcements. They don't know you, so that means you didn't find Excalibur!"

"Excalibur is my sword, Merlin! I have to get it. This is my destiny!" the teenage boy retorts, his face darkening.

"Wait!" Liam jumps in, startling both the boy and the wizard. "Are you Lancelot?"

The teenage boy gasps. "I am Arthur! The future King of England!" he shouts in despair before turning to Merlin. "Everything is your fault!" Arthur crosses his arms over his chest and starts to sulk.

"Don't say that, Arthur! We'll fix it, I promise, my boy!" Merlin tells him, taking him by the shoulders. Aria and Liam exchange a worried glance, unsure of what is happening.

"Now they've come, everything will be alright!" Merlin continues, staring at them as if willing them to take action. Aria gazes at Liam, who looks just as confused as she does.

"You promised I would be king!" Arthur sobs, still with his back to the wizard.

"And you will, my sweet boy!" Merlin retorts in a sweet, confident voice. "Our friends right here will find Excalibur for you!"

Liam breaks out in nervous laughter, wondering if he's lost his mind since hitting his head against Aria's, as he chortles, "What on earth is he talking about?" glancing over at Aria, whose gaze is fixed on Merlin and the boy.

Arthur abruptly spins around. He steps closer to Liam, threatening him with his finger. "Do you think this is amusing? I am Arthur, the future monarch of

England, and if you don't find *my* Excalibur and give it to me, I will…"

"Do what? Kill us with whining?" Aria inquires, making Liam burst into laughter.

"Well said, my dear Aria!" Liam manages to wheeze.

Arthur shakes with rage, unable to process her words. "Merlin will cast a spell on you!" he finally yells, waving his arms around menacingly.

"I thought you said his magic was not up to standard lately," Aria retorts.

Arthur's face is bright red as he turns to the old man. "Merlin! What idiots have you brought here?" he screams, his fist clenched against his sides.

"Arthur, calm down, my son," Merlin softly replies as he pats the boy on the back. Then he turns to stare at Aria. "I expect you to be respectful toward my boy. I didn't bring you to make matters worse than they already are."

"I'm sorry, but your problems aren't our concern," Liam jumps in.

"That's not entirely true," Merlin replies. "Until you accomplish your mission here, you won't be able to return to your own time."

Aria and Liam stare helplessly at each other as Arthur glares. Without giving them time to object,

Merlin turns and heads off through the tranquil forest, with its soft shadows dappled with sunrays. The trees, of various shapes and sizes, look ancient. Nothing is regular or even, but everything looks so balanced and peaceful.

Aria and Liam reluctantly follow Arthur and Merlin, as the wizard uses his walking stick to test a safe path on the muddy ground. After a few minutes of silence, Merlin starts to explain the events that led to their appearance in this place and time.

It all began seventeen years ago, when Merlin foresaw the turmoil that would come after Uther Pendragon, the King of England, died without a clear heir. With his magical powers, Merlin helped Uther and Igraine meet, and soon after, baby Arthur was born. But Arthur was taken away to be raised secretly to keep him safe from Uther's enemies until he was ready to claim his birthright. Under Merlin's guidance and teachings, Arthur would become the perfect ruler and bring forth a golden age in Britain. When his father died, Arthur would have to find Excalibur and draw it from its stone to be crowned King of England.

"That was a nice tale, but I'm afraid I've never heard of this Arthur character. Have you, Aria?" Liam interrupts.

"Liam, who knew you were so good in history?" Aria responds happily before looking at Merlin and Arthur. "I am afraid Liam is right. No Arthur made history."

Merlin stops to look at them, while Arthur glowers murderously beside him. "That is why you are here. You must help Arthur find Excalibur so he can rightfully take the throne."

"Doesn't he have to find it himself for it to work?" Aria asks. "At least that's what Lancelot did to become king…"

"I cannot find it! It has been hidden," Arthur yells. "And don't mention Lancelot again. I am the one who should be king!"

Merlin moves closer to Arthur, putting his hand on the boy's back to soothe him.

"You see, we don't know where Excalibur is," the old man explains.

"And you want us to find it?" Liam asks, as he looks at the vast forest surrounding them.

"That's right!" Merlin says brightly.

"But aren't you the one who hid it?" Aria wonders. "At least, that's what the history books say."

Arthur shoots an exasperated glance upward, making Merlin look ashamed.

"I did…" the old man begins. "But you see, some people want to prevent Arthur from becoming king, so they moved it."

"I wonder why," Liam mutters.

"As you search for Excalibur, you will face the forces of darkness," Merlin continues, ignoring Liam's sarcasm.

"What do you mean?" Aria asks.

Merlin's piercing gaze met Aria's, his voice steady and serious, "The most powerful society in England, the Circle of Druids, will do everything to stop us from finding Excalibur. They are determined to see us fail. They've hidden Excalibur to make sure Arthur can never become King. And by doing that, they will make this country fall."

CHAPTER 3
MERLIN'S TALE

As the sun reaches its zenith, the group arrives at a small clearing, in the middle of which stands a small but cozy cottage with a thatched roof. It's perched on a small bluff, and flowers of all colors surround it. A billowing column of hazy smoke floats upward from the chimney, wafting an unfamiliar fragrance around the clearing.

Aria and Liam look around in bewilderment. Liam gives Aria a nudge to get her attention and gestures toward the left side of the house, where a cabin as tiny as a broom cupboard with a pointed roof and a wooden door with a gold handle stands. In front of it is a massive cauldron suspended over what appears to be a burnt-out fire. Cauldrons of various sizes dangle from the nearby tree like pans in a kitchen.

"Do you think that's where he makes his potions?" Aria asks, amazed at the sight.

Liam rolls his eyes before responding, "This isn't a movie, Aria. I don't think he's actually a magician."

"My dear Liam, how do you think we are able to travel through time if it's not thanks to magic?"

Caught off guard, Liam pauses, his mind racing. The mechanics of their time travel had always been a mystery; they only knew it happened when they were called upon to help someone. "Perhaps there's a hint of magic in our travels, Aria," Liam concedes softly, a new thoughtfulness softening his voice. "But even if it is magic, it's a far cry from potion-making!" He looks at her, his expression a mix of bewilderment and awe.

Merlin paces toward the big cauldron and with a snap of his fingers rekindles the fire. Liam stares in wonder at the flames that seemingly erupt from thin air, licking the sides of the cauldron. He squints as he looks around, trying to figure out how Merlin ignited the fire so quickly.

"Shall we enter?" Merlin inquires with a smile.

"I'm going in! I'm a bit tired, so I think I'll take a nap," Arthur replies. He walks straight inside the big house without waiting for anyone else.

"Go ahead, my boy!" Merlin shouts after him. "He's had a rough morning," he explains to the others. "Shall we?" With a gesture, he invites Aria and Liam inside.

The adventurers enter a cozy room with ample natural light pouring in through the windows. In the center of the room stands a small wooden table surrounded by four chairs, while at one side near the fireplace are two armchairs upholstered with wool. They can't help but admire the unusual decor— paintings of Arthur looking noble, and bizarrely shaped rocks arranged to look like cats and dogs. Various necklaces crafted from plants and stones hang on the wall, making the room even more eccentric.

"Please, take a seat," Merlin offers, removing wooden swords and clothes from two chairs. "Arthur can be a little bit messy!"

"A little bit?" Liam inquires skeptically.

"You said druids might be behind Excalibur's disappearance?" Aria asks, urgency in her voice.

Merlin gives a light smile, then heaves a heavy sigh. "When I used my magic to arrange the meeting between Uther and Igraine, it was with a specific purpose—to save England from chaos. In my vision, I saw how the country would be thrown into disarray unless there was a clear successor to the throne. Far too many men wanted what only one man could get. Thus, with Arthur's birth, all was set right. Unfortunately, the Circle of Druids disapproved of this solution, wanting someone other than him to lead the kingdom."

"Lancelot!" Aria cuts in, her eyes aglow.

"Exactly!" Merlin confirms.

"But why do they want Lancelot more than Arthur?" Liam asks, puzzled.

Merlin pauses for a moment before continuing. "The Circle of Druids is convinced by an old prophecy that claims a king, raised by a wizard, will bring destruction upon the kingdom through his dark and wicked alliances. As the best druid in England, I was their major target before they began to disrupt my magical abilities. That is why we kept Arthur hidden. However, one day, they discovered his existence, and it became a priority for them to eliminate us."

"But why not have him raised by someone else if you knew about the prophecy?" Liam wonders.

"Because I could not guarantee his education! I never dreamed they would actually believe the prophecy. I thought I could protect him and raise him like a true king without anyone finding out!"

"Well, you definitely made him act like a king," Aria jokes.

Merlin looks at her before continuing, pretending to be unaffected by her scorn. "Arthur only had to find Excalibur and draw it from the stone to claim his throne—but I did not expect the Circle to discover it! I cast this spell in secret. Now they have managed to conceal the sword and are attempting to strip me of my powers," he continues in frustration. "I had to cast a spell all over the house so they would not find us!"

Aria gives him a sympathetic look. Even if Arthur is the most entitled person she's ever encountered, she can tell how much Merlin cares about him. And she knows the historical consequences of Lancelot's rule.

"What's wrong?" Liam inquires, seeing fear in her eyes.

She quickly glances at him before her eyes dart

back to Merlin. He seems to guess what she's thinking.

"I think we should help them," she declares.

"I didn't know we had a choice," Liam retorts.

"Hear me out," she goes on. "I know Arthur is, er…"

"Spoiled? Full of himself? Capricious?"

Aria nods. "Yes, yes, and yes, and maybe many more things! But don't forget what happened to England after Lancelot was crowned king."

Liam scrunches up his face, striving to recall the end of the story. He remembered being struck by the bravery and strength it took to pull the sword Excalibur from the stone, but he hadn't paid much attention to what came afterward.

Before he can admit that he doesn't know the answer, Aria begins one of her famous history monologues. "Lancelot managed to remove Excalibur from the stone and returned to Camelot with it. Despite his victory, he was seen as a pretender to the throne because he had no royal blood. Moreover, his mistrust of others led him to rule alone, preferring to make all his decisions without consulting anyone. It didn't take long for neighboring countries to attack and seize control."

At her words, Merlin's eyes fill with tears. "All my life's efforts come to nothing?"

"Alright, I understand, but we don't know what will happen if Arthur takes the throne, correct?" Liam inquires. Aria nods. "And why did they choose Lancelot if he is such a bad king?" he continues. "Don't they have some kind of psychic power like you?"

"No, I am the only druid alive with visions of the future. I tried to convince them, but they did not want to believe my vision!" Merlin exclaims in despair.

"Okay, but given Arthur's attitude, I'm not sure he's up to the task," Liam adds.

"He is! I guarantee you I have been preparing him to be a great ruler," Merlin interjects eagerly.

A distant cry from Arthur interrupts them. "Merlin! Bring me a cup of fruited nectar brew!" he yells from inside his chambers.

"Do you think you could say please?" Merlin softly asks.

"What did you say?" Arthur demands as he joins them. "I need something to drink!" Merlin springs to his feet and strides across the room to the fireplace. With a snap of his fingers, he brings the flames back to life.

In the meantime, Liam turns to Aria and begs her, "Can you make him your special hot chocolate so we can get some peace and quiet?" Aria giggles at the memory of how she once got out of a particularly sticky situation using a clever trick— hot chocolate with a very sleepy ingredient inside.

Merlin smiles and holds out a steaming cup to Arthur, who takes his place on the rough-hewn chair. "Enjoy this brew, my boy!" Merlin says cheerfully.

Liam scrutinizes Arthur, then looks back to the wizard. "Okay, so we have to find Excalibur, but how? If you didn't manage to find it, how can we?"

"The Circle of Druids has drawn up a map for Lancelot," Merlin explains.

"So, our first mission is to track down the map," Aria says.

Arthur swiftly stands up, dropping droplets of fruited nectar brew in the process. "No! We need to follow Lancelot and…"

"What? Attack him as he's standing in front of the stone?" Liam exclaims in exasperation.

Arthur's face brightens at the idea. "Yes, that is a good plan!"

Aria and Liam stay silent for a minute. The idea of this teenager becoming a great king seems impossible.

"We're adventurers, not gangsters," Liam finally speaks.

"He's right," says Aria. "We can't do that. And how will you win people's hearts if you steal something without earning it?"

Arthur looks at them in disbelief. He is destined for the throne; Excalibur is his sword.

"You are right," Merlin intervenes. "We will need to retrieve the map from the druids first."

Arthur's eyes widen in confusion. "What exactly do you mean by 'we'?"

"Do you think we're going to search for the sword that could make you king alone?" Liam demands, astonished.

"Yes, that is your job!" Arthur snaps back.

"If it's my job, let me make one thing clear: if I manage to find Excalibur, I'll be the one who wears the crown!" Liam warns, grinning slightly at Aria. She can't help but think he wouldn't be too bad as a ruler.

"Son..." Merlin steps in, trying to diffuse the tension. "You must come with us. It's the only way to win the crown. That's how I cast the spell."

Arthur exhales in frustration. He would have chosen to stay in his chambers all day rather than venturing into the woods again; they always give him a pounding headache. "If I must go, I will," he says reluctantly, "but you better find it quickly!"

"We will!" Merlin cheers, though Aria and Liam don't share his enthusiasm. The old druid scurries toward the door as quickly as he can. He grasps the handle firmly—

—when an explosion shatters the peace outside.

CHAPTER 4
A PINCH OF MAGIC

Thick green smoke appears at the window. Merlin's eyes light up at the sight, and a smile spreads across his face. He quickly clasps his hands and dashes out, to the surprise of the others.

Merlin trots toward the bubbling cauldron at the corner of the cottage. Aria and Liam rush after him while Arthur takes his time. A sudden explosion of boiling green liquid makes everyone jump in surprise.

"What is it?" Liam asks, wrinkling his nose at the smell.

"That, my friend, is one of my best concoctions: a vigor elixir!" Merlin's face lights up with joy, which is replaced by a look of disgust when a new explosion splatters his white beard with green goo.

"It looks…delicious." Aria winces.

"You are going to get some, but first I have to perform a ritual to locate the Circle of Druids' village," Merlin announces as he hastens toward the mysterious cabin.

Liam stares at Aria in disbelief. It seems that what they've experienced so far is only the start of something far more bizarre than they could ever imagine. He remembers learning about the story of Lancelot and his adventures with the Knights of the Round Table during school. But what if Merlin's tale is true? And since when was magic real? The information jumbles up and clashes in his head, making him even more confused.

"You're about to be proven wrong, my dear Liam," Aria insists. In her opinion, Liam can be way too rational. He never wants to believe that legends or folklore are true, despite all the inexplicable events they've experienced during their adventures.

Merlin staggers out of his cabin, his arms loaded with peculiar items: stones, talismans, leaves, and various herbs. He sets it all down on the trunk of a felled tree that serves as a seat. The druid takes a moment to inspect his treasures while rubbing his chin, his eyebrows furrowed.

Then he starts and makes a surprised sound before smiling and racing back into his cabin. He soon reappears, clutching a blue crystal, which he places near the other items.

Liam breaks the silence by asking, "What are you doing exactly?"

Merlin grins at him with a twinkle in his eye. "I'm getting ready to cast my spell! Do you really think we have time to search the entire forest for the village?"

"But don't you know where the druids live?" Aria asks, befuddled.

"I used to, but it's been quite a while since I broke contact with the circle and moved here. My recollection isn't that strong…" He sighs.

"They never came to see you or try to fix the situation?"

"Aria, you really don't listen," Liam scolds. "He told us he had to hide from them so they wouldn't take Arthur!" He is clearly happy to be the one on top of things for once.

"I see you are listening, my boy." Merlin grins before peering at Aria, who is failing to conceal her irritation. "I had to secure this place so they would not locate us. Arthur's protection is the main priority, so I cast a spell around the house that makes us invisible. The Circle attempted to find us, but they were unsuccessful. They tried to reduce my magical powers with some spells, but I remained stronger than them," he declares proudly.

Liam and Aria refrain from commenting. They now understand why Arthur is the way he is.

"But don't they have a way of detecting when someone uses magic?" Aria finally asks, remembering Celtic legends.

Merlin is startled at finding her so knowledgeable. "Excellent question!" he congratulates her, making her hop in excitement. "They cannot detect the magic I do inside the circle!" he explains before raising his finger and rushing back into his cabin.

Liam moves closer to the tree trunk, eager to get a better look at the mysterious items. Without hesitation, he reaches out his hand and carefully touches them.

"Liam!" Aria protests. "What are you doing now!"

Liam gets to his feet and examines her closely before raising his gaze and shielding his eyes with his hand.

"What? What's the matter?" Aria searches around.

"I'm searching for your curiosity, my dear Aria! You're usually the one sticking your nose where it doesn't belong!"

Aria's face contorts as she sighs. "Very funny, my dear Liam!"

Merlin reappears, waving his hands in the air as if he has just finished washing them. "I am ready," the druid declares as he pushes his magician's robe behind him. He rolls up his sleeves before raising his fingers. His gaze settles on one of the talismans. He grabs it and slips it around his neck, then swiftly picks up the crystal and places it on a tree trunk. He rotates his index finger above the rest of the objects before grabbing a pine branch and a sprig of mistle-toe. Without hesitating, he passes the branch and the sprig to the bewildered adventurers.

"Um…" Liam begins, looking at the mistletoe in his hand. "What are we supposed to do with this?"

Merlin pauses in his frenzied preparations and gazes at them. "Perform the ritual; what do you think?" he responds as if this were the most normal thing in the world. "Come on, my friends, stand in a circle around the trunk!"

Aria and Liam take their positions, feeling

their hearts thumping faster. Mingled exhilaration and trepidation sweep through them as their hands start to shake, still gripping the ceremonial items.

Merlin picks up the last object from the trunk and then looks around. "Arthur! Arthur, my boy, where are you?" he calls softly as he roams the area in search of his adopted child.

Liam leans toward Aria, the mistletoe branch held high in the air away from their faces. "If he goes missing, it won't be a huge deal," he jokes.

"We'd have to go looking for him, and that doesn't sound like a fun time," Aria points out, making Liam shudder. He hadn't considered that.

Liam begins to yell Arthur's name, his bellows a sharp contrast to Merlin's tranquil voice. Eventually Arthur peers down from a tree, where he has evidently been sleeping.

"I've found him!" Liam bellows.

Merlin scampers up, a relieved smile on his face. "Ah, there you are! I've been searching for you all over! We need you to perform the ritual."

Arthur stirs grumpily, still half-asleep. "You could've been more gentle!" he mumbles as he stretches his limbs and climbs down from the tree.

"Maybe you'd like some treats?" Liam scoffs.

Arthur looks up and rubs his lips before replying, "Why not? I'm kind of hungry!"

Liam stares at him, taken aback by his response, while Aria laughs.

"Let's go! We must hurry if we want to start our journey soon," Merlin urges.

The four quickly gather around the trunk where the crystal is sitting on top. After ensuring that Aria, Liam, and Arthur are holding their respective branches over it, Merlin closes his eyes. The others watch uncertainly as his face relaxes and he takes a deep breath. He extends his arms outwards and begins to move them in a circular motion as he takes an even deeper breath. A light wind starts up at the group's feet, causing fallen leaves to flutter. When the wind gets faster, Liam's expression turns worried while Aria's is filled with delight. When the breeze becomes a whirlwind Merlin, keeping his eyes firmly closed, begins to chant loudly, authoritative and self-assured:

"Golden strands of Awen's grace,
Reveal the hidden druidic space!
Through wood and hill, let light entwine,
Trace the path to the circle divine!"

When he finishes chanting, Merlin's eyes fly open. His fingers tightly grasp the talisman around his neck, and a spark of golden lightning shoots out toward the branches held by the group. All three jump in surprise as the wood bursts into flames. The objects slip from their grasp before turning into golden dust and falling into the shining crystal. They gape in shock as a golden filament emerges from the crystal, winding its way high above the ground.

⚊

A MAN with a long brown beard and hair of the same color stares at a text inscribed on a stone. His blue velvet robe almost drags on the floor as he hikes up his sleeves so they don't get in the way as he writes.

Suddenly, a crystal that sits beneath a glass dome on top of a wooden chest behind the desk begins to shine. Its glow increases until it is too bright for the druid to look at directly. His eyes widen with shock, and he lets out a loud gasp, quickly scrambling to his feet before sprinting outside.

He soon arrives at the largest building in the village. Without waiting for permission, he rushes inside and halts, out of breath. A dozen men and women, each of a certain age and dressed in long emerald robes adorned with golden symbols signifying nature's balance, stare at him intently.

"Merlin! Merlin…" the bearded man stammers, trying to catch his breath. "He has done magic!"

The leader of the Circle of Druids stands up in surprise, a look of anger mixed with terror spreading across his face.

CHAPTER 5

THE CIRCLE OF DRUIDS

T he Circle of Druids is stunned into silence as the man who has just delivered the news struggles to catch his breath after the unexpected run.

The leader of the council, Tanglewood, stares at the assembly, the long white hair surrounding his wrinkled face turning electric. One of the oldest and most knowledgeable druids in the Circle, he has been around long enough to know Merlin very well. But he had never expected that he would one day have to battle an old friend. Though he foresaw this day, given what happened the last time they spoke, a part of him had hoped they would never have to face each other.

"Thank you, Leafrunner, for coming so quickly to alert us," Tanglewood finally says.

A woman with grey hair and intense green eyes asks, "Do you think he is looking for Excalibur?" She and Tanglewood were close companions of Merlin when they all attended the druid school. Their bond was so strong that their teachers often referred to them as a single person.

Tanglewood replies sadly, "I'm afraid so, Faewind."

"We need to go after him and Arthur and put a stop to this," insists one of the younger druids.

Faewind stares at him with desperation in her eyes. Even though Merlin has caused trouble lately, they can't resort to using evil forces against him. It's against druidic law. She gets up and declares, "That's not an option!"

"Faewind, stay calm. They do not know him like we do!" Tanglewood reminds her.

"Yes, and that's why we should make the decision," another druid interjects. "You are too involved in this. But we need to protect England at all costs. We cannot let him put Arthur on the throne!"

Tanglewood glances at each of the druids in the room, making them shiver. It's the first time that such a serious matter has been brought up to the

Circle, which usually only deals with daily administrative matters. Tanglewood does not need to speak to command, the pressure of his gaze on each of them in turn effective enough as he paces in the room.

"You think you will just be able to attack Merlin, and he will collapse?" Tanglewood inquires. "Then let me tell you: you are fools!"

"You managed to hide Excalibur. You must know how to stop him," one of the druids retorts.

Tanglewood comes to a halt in front of the druid who spoke up. "Faewind and I were able to conceal Excalibur together. She will tell you that underestimating Merlin will not secure us a victory."

"He is right," Faewind intervenes. "Merlin has always been the most powerful of us. We should focus on helping Lancelot find Excalibur first. Once he has it, even Merlin will be unable to question his right to the crown!"

The druids start murmuring amongst themselves, debating the proposal. After considering their options, one finally says, "You are correct. We should send someone to Lancelot right away with the map so he can find Excalibur before Arthur does. Do they have the map?"

"Not that we know of. But even if we have cast

the spell so no magic can help find Excalibur, Merlin's power is immense. He may still find a work-around," Faewind cautions.

"Leafrunner will find Lancelot. Faewind and I will prepare a surprise for Merlin. Their journey in the forest will be more challenging than they expect; you will see," Tanglewood adds, a furtive smile on his face. Faewind looks at him. In a brisk second, she reads his mind and chuckles at what she sees. With the incantation she and Tanglewood have cast, Merlin and his friend will never find the sword. If they manage to leave the forest, that itself will be a remarkable feat.

After giving instructions to an overjoyed Leafrunner, Tanglewood heads out with Faewind.

As he reaches the door, one of the druids calls over to him, "Don't forget that if this fails, we will need to escalate our actions." Tanglewood nods in silence, confident in his plan.

Leafrunner trembles as he rushes out of the reception room. This is the first time he's been entrusted with such an important task since arriving in the village. He grins, skipping with joy as he hurries back to his office. There's no time to waste. He has to get ready for the mission of his life!

THE THIN GOLD filament stretches on into infinity. Liam's hand trembles as he points out the flying strand. "Aria, do you see it?" he whispers.

Aria's eyes sparkle as she stares at the magical filament. She has never seen anything so spectacular. "This is magic!" she shouts, jumping in excitement.

Liam frowns. "That can't be true," he mutters, unable to believe his eyes. "Magic doesn't exist."

"Come on, my dear Liam. You're seeing it with your own eyes," Aria teases him. "And you saw Merlin light the fire with his finger!"

Liam touches the base of his neck, grimacing. "I thought he had a match stashed somewhere. I don't know, like in a magician's show," he exclaims, baffled.

Merlin brags triumphantly, "I am a magician, just as I said!"

"So, are we going now, or do we have to wait for him to pull himself together?" Arthur asks, pointing at Liam, whose face is pale with shock.

Merlin rushes to his cabin, quickly returning with wooden cups. "I have exactly what you need!" he exclaims before taking a ladle from the still-boiling cauldron. He quickly fills the cups and passes them to the adventurers and Arthur. Aria and Liam eye the bubbling green liquid with suspicion, but Arthur takes a sip without hesitation, then drains his cup in a single gulp and sighs contentedly.

"What is *this*?" Liam asks, scowling at the green liquid.

"That's the *vigor elixir*, my dear Liam! Merlin told us earlier. You'd know if you had listened!" She jabs at him playfully, then takes a deep breath and gulps down the entire contents of her cup. Her face scrunches at the unexpectedly sour taste.

Liam glances at her nervously. Her expression isn't encouraging.

"So, how do you like it?" Merlin demands.

"Holy guacamole!" Aria cries out. "That's one heck of a cocktail!"

"I am glad you like it. Sometimes, I think it lacks a bit of salt," Merlin admits.

"Salt?" Liam queries.

"Come on, my dear Liam, drink it! You'll love it!" Aria urges him.

"Drink it!" Arthur echoes in a sudden burst of enthusiasm.

Aria and Arthur start chanting, "Drink it! Drink it! Drink it!" as they jump up and down in front of Liam, who watches in bewilderment. Finally, to shut them up, Liam brings the cup to his lips and gulps down its contents.

"That's disgusting!" he exclaims. When Merlin regards him resentfully, Liam regrets his reaction, quickly composes himself and declares, "No, that's not what I meant! It's fantastic... I–I was surprised by how sour it tasted..." he stammers as Merlin's expression does not change. "The best drink I've ever had! A real punch in the face!" He laughs awkwardly.

"Look at me! I'm feeling so energized!" Aria cries as she jumps up and down.

Liam is astounded when he feels the same energy surging through his own limbs. "Me too!" he cries, and finds himself hopping for no reason. It's usually Aria, a professional hyperactive, who does that, while he tells her to calm down.

"That's normal for a vigor elixir! It is meant to give you a punch of energy," Merlin explains.

"Maybe too much of a punch." Arthur raises his eyebrows at Aria and Liam as they continue jumping around.

"It won't have the same impact on you, my boy. You're too accustomed to it!" Merlin retorts.

"Let's go!" Liam cries, unable to contain his excitement.

The two adventurers follow the line of the gold filament, bounding instead of strolling along. Merlin watches them, delighted. They will need all their energy for what awaits them in the woods.

Merlin realizes that by casting this specific enchantment, he has breached the safety bubble he cast many years ago. The Circle of Druids must already have sensed his spell. Knowing them, they will do everything they can to stop him from finding Excalibur. Merlin and the children must remain vigilant and prepared for any possible attack.

As they walk away from the clearing, a blanket of fog slowly covers the woods. The adventurers' excited cries mingle with the cawing of the crows. Merlin's expression darkens, his right hand tightly gripping the handle of his cane.

CHAPTER 6

THE MAP TO EXCALIBUR

Aria and Liam skip happily through the woods, following the gold filament, thrilled at this new adventure. The fog around their feet quickly rises to knee level. Arthur lags behind as his adoptive father's elixir has lost its effect on him. Merlin walks cautiously behind them, unwilling to strain his aged legs.

"You two, could you please slow down?" Arthur calls out as the mist gets thicker.

Liam pauses for a moment, and his eyes sparkle as he grins. "If you can't keep up by walking, run!" he advises before hurrying on.

"At last, you see my point, my dear Liam!" Aria exclaims, happy that he can keep up with her for once.

"True, my dear Aria. It's fun to be hyperactive!" Liam dodges an enormous tree root.

Aria and Liam both smile as they hurry on. Although there's a lovely glimmer of fading sunlight, the thickening fog slowly covers their legs, making it almost impossible to see where they are stepping or jumping.

Suddenly Aria lands on a sharp stone, tumbles face-first to the ground, and disappears in the fog. Liam stops abruptly just a few steps behind her.

"Aria!" he exclaims, wondering if this is another of Merlin's magic tricks. "Aria!" he calls out again, panic rising.

A faint "I'm here!" breaks through the fog as her hand emerges from the mist.

Liam laughs before rushing to rescue her.

A strangled squeak escapes her lips as Liam steps on her foot, which is hidden in the mist. "Oh, sorry!" he exclaims before reaching down to help her up. She stands up straight and dusts off her sweater.

Eventually, Arthur catches up with them. "Some adventurers," he mocks. Aria and Liam scowl.

"If you're disappointed, we can leave you and Merlin to manage this mission yourselves," Aria retorts, looking around for the old druid. But he's nowhere in sight.

Arthur grits his teeth before deciding not to reply. Even though he loves his adoptive father deeply, Merlin is in no physical state to fight the Circle of Druids.

Aria and Liam stare at Arthur, waiting for an answer. As they are about to move away, Liam freezes, gaping.

Aria raises her eyebrows. "What is it?" she asks.

"Look!" Liam cries, pointing at a tree. Aria and Arthur look in the direction he indicates, but don't see anything special. Arthur shakes his head and complains, "I don't see anything!"

"Trust me, it's right in front of the big branch at the top of the trunk," Liam says.

Puzzled, Aria squints to get a better look. "You mean that little wooden birdhouse?"

"Yes!" Liam cries. "Isn't it beautiful?" Aria and Arthur gape at him. Apparently, the potion didn't just energize him, it turned him sentimental too.

"Yes, wonderful, my dear Liam," Aria responds in a condescending tone.

"I'm sure it's very nice," says Arthur, "but let's stay focused on our mission." He sets off again.

Liam shakes his head in disbelief. *How can they not*

be amazed by such enchantment? he wonders before setting off behind the others.

"So, what was it like to be raised by someone like Merlin?" Aria asks Arthur.

Arthur smiles faintly as he stares at the gold filament. "It was great! He knows how to entertain kids with magic." Then he laughs at Liam and Aria's surprised expressions. This is the first time they've heard him sound affectionate or playful. "Though things were less fun after Merlin had to seal us in the bubble," Arthur adds.

"How were things before?" Liam asks.

Arthur gazes at him in surprise. They don't know much, for people who are supposed to be from the future. "I was around ten years old when it happened. Merlin arrived home from a meeting with the Circle of Druids and immediately began constructing a protective dome around the house. He was furious; I had never seen him in such a state." As Arthur speaks, mist gradually swirls around his feet, becoming denser with each passing moment.

"Why didn't you need the bubble before? I thought the Circle were against you taking the throne from the moment you were born?" Aria asks.

"You really don't know anything!" Arthur

exclaims and gives a long sigh. "No, they changed their minds. After that happened, I wasn't allowed to go far from the house. Before, it was lonely, but I could go hunting. It was so much fun!" He smirks as Aria and Liam wince at the idea of hunting animals.

They try to think of what it would be like to live without their friends. It sounds so horrible they don't know what to say.

"Don't get me wrong, Merlin did everything he could to cheer me up. He never refused me anything," Arthur adds, seeing their pitying looks.

Liam turns to smirk at Aria. "That explains why he's so spoiled," he whispers, making Aria laugh quietly.

"That's not an excuse! My father never refused me anything, and I'm not like that," Aria whispers back.

Liam grits his teeth and gives a forced-looking smile. Aria nudges him, understanding precisely what he means.

"Come on, I'm joking!" Liam exclaims, and bursts into laughter.

Their laughter fades when Arthur stops in his tracks.

LEAFRUNNER TAPS his horse's belly to quicken his pace. He only has a little time to accomplish his mission. He must find Lancelot as quickly as possible.

After riding through the forest, he eventually arrives at Camelot. He pulls back on his horse's reins and stops to pass through the guarded gates.

As he enters the bustling town, it's almost impossible to dodge all the people hurrying up and down the main street. Farmers carry bales of hay and food, blacksmiths are hard at work sharpening swords, and a group gathers around a baker to purchase some fresh bread. The Circle of Druids village is much calmer and more organized.

After a few minutes of riding his horse through the city, he stops at an inn. People are gathered there, sipping on beers and enjoying bread and vegetables. Leafrunner heads to the bar, where the bartender is wiping down a glass.

"Sorry to bother you, but I'm looking for someone. Can you help me?" he asks shyly.

The man's muscular figure makes the druid nervous. The bartender sets the glass aside and stares into his eyes. "And who are you looking for?" he asks, bracing his arm on the counter.

"Um… Lancelot," the druid replies, trying to sound casual.

The man smiles faintly as he observes the stranger's peculiar clothes. "I hope you don't mean him any harm?"

"No! No! On the contrary!" Leafrunner cries.

The bartender gestures behind him. "You're in luck. He's behind you." Leafrunner turns and spots a solitary individual sitting at a table not far away.

Lancelot is dressed in a gray tunic and brown hunting pants, his light brown hair cascading past his shoulders. The druid walks hesitantly over, before summoning the courage to tap him on the shoulder. As Lancelot turns around, his blue eyes sparkle, and he gives a reassuring grin. Leafrunner is immediately comforted.

"Yes, what can I do for you?" Lancelot asks in a jovial tone with a pinch of condescension as he regards the druid's outfit.

"Do you want to become the next King of England?" Leafrunner asks boldly, his eyes wide and his voice mysterious.

Lancelot's breath catches as he examines Leafrunner closely. The druid then reaches into his robe and pulls a scroll of paper out of a pocket. Hands shaking, Lancelot takes the parchment from him. "This is the map to your destiny!" Leafrunner tells him with a solemn expression. "Don't disappoint the Circle of Druids!"

With that, the druid rushes out of the inn, leaving a bewildered Lancelot sitting in his chair with the map in his hand.

CHAPTER 7

THE INVISIBLE CREATURE

S itting cross-legged in the middle of a dimly lit room, Tanglewood and Faewind cast their spell. A whirlwind spins around them. When the final word is spoken, light streams from a pink stone between them. It fills every corner of the room until it is replaced by a cloud of smoke, gracefully spinning and twirling in the air before flowing out through an open window. The two druids observe as the fog dwindles into the distance, dark and murky, before finally blending into the trees on the outskirts of the village.

"Do you think we have done too much?" Faewind asks Tanglewood as she stands up, looking at the heavy mist invading the forest.

Tanglewood joins her at the window. "No, we

need to stop them, whatever it takes," he replies as he grasps her shoulder to reassure her. "It will not kill them. Don't worry. It will only slow them down."

"You are right," Faewind says, still watching the mist. "I know Merlin did something wrong, but... but he is..." she stammers.

"One of our oldest friends," Tanglewood completes her sentence. "I know."

Faewind turns deliberately to face her companion, her eyes sharp and discerning. "Perhaps we should observe them discreetly to ensure the plan's efficacy," she suggests with gravity.

Tanglewood replies, "Perhaps you are right. Let's get our paws into this business!" he exclaims before raising his right hand. A snap of his fingers is all it takes for him to transform into a black cat with piercing yellow eyes. Faewind quickly follows suit, and the felines jump out the window and head for the woods.

ARTHUR GLARES AHEAD, then grinds his teeth and growls.

"What is it?" Liam asks. Aria glances around, searching for the cause of Arthur's rage, yet everything seems tranquil. The trees sway gently with the breeze, their leaves rustling in an almost calming rhythm.

Arthur slides his dagger from its belt with a controlled but determined movement and holds it out in front of him. He takes a step forward, his face hardening.

Aria and Liam glance around nervously, not knowing which way the danger is coming from. Without speaking, Arthur slowly advances toward a nearby tree.

"What's the matter?" Aria pleads, her eyes darting around in confusion.

"Are you blind or what?" Arthur speaks quietly, his right arm still in a defensive posture with the dagger tightly grasped. Liam frowns, wondering what he's talking about.

Arthur stalks forward, back hunched and knees bent, finally pointing a trembling finger at the tree. "The bear!" he cries.

Aria glances at Liam in confusion. "Can you see anything?" she asks.

"No! There's nothing. He's lost his head!" Liam stares blankly.

"I think Merlin must have added something unusual to his potion," Aria suggests.

Arthur shrieks as he jumps to his feet, brandishing his dagger and sprinting toward the tree. Aria and Liam are taken aback as the boy stabs the air. After a few minutes of frantic action, Arthur finally stops and catches his breath before wiping the sweat from his forehead with his shirt sleeve.

"No need to thank me," he declares sternly as the pair stare in disbelief.

"For what?" Aria inquires archly.

Arthur looks at them in disbelief. "For saving your life from the bear! You two really need to brush up your skills if you want to be useful during this mission. I am not doing all the work alone. So pay more attention!"

Liam and Aria are too stunned to speak. Arthur spins around and begins to stride back toward the gold filament. Liam finally speaks up, turning to Aria with an incredulous look on his face. "Can you believe that guy?"

"He's got some nerve! He wants to be rewarded for battling an imaginary creature!"

Liam laughs. "We better keep an eye on him. Who knows, he might see an invisible Excalibur!"

"At least that'll spare England from having such a spoiled king!" Aria adds with a grin before turning serious. "Where is Merlin, by the way?"

Liam turns around and raises his head to search for the old druid. At last, he spots Merlin's emerald robe, with its eye-catching golden hems. "There!" he exclaims pointing. "He's so slow."

"Don't tell me! But we also need to keep an eye on him. There's something fishy about his story. Either he or Arthur are lying, because their tales don't match," Aria reminds him.

"You're right. I think I trust Arthur more," Liam confesses, making Aria's eyes widen with surprise. "It's just, Arthur is younger, so he might have a better memory than Merlin," he explains, making Aria smile. "But let's keep that secret. I don't want Merlin to turn me into a pig!" Liam winces.

Aria bellows with laughter, tears in her eyes. "You'll make such a beautiful pig!" she teases as they move forward.

Merlin takes his time, strolling along at the back of the group. The solitude allows him to savor the environment around him. It's been ages since he had the chance to revel in the fragrance of the plants, watching them swaying in the breeze. In the forest, he can recall his teacher at the druids' school telling him about the importance of balance in nature and life. It brings back the old memories of his two best friends, Tanglewood and Faewind, playing hide-and-seek between classes. They only wanted to race through the woods and cast quirky spells as they went. A gentle smile crosses his face. Today, he has nothing but his memories.

A shrill scream jolts him from his daydreaming. He quickens his pace to catch up with the rest of the group.

Aria stands apart from them, pointing to a mysterious rock shrouded in a thick blanket of fog. "Look! I found it!" she cries, jumping up and down, unable to control herself.

Liam steps closer, his eyes on a large, faceted rock on the ground. It's big enough to sit on, but there's nothing extraordinary about it. He looks at Aria in confusion. "What did you find?"

Arthur soon arrives, looking just as perplexed as Liam. Aria's eyes sparkle energetically as she gestures at the large rock, her cheeks flushing with eagerness. As neither of the boys give any sign of sharing her excitement, her expression sags, her frustration mounting. "Are you guys blind? Don't you see?" she insists, her arms turning rigid at her sides.

"We aren't blind," Liam retorts. "You, my dear Aria, have eaten something that's made you lose your mind!"

"I am not crazy!" Aria shouts before spinning

around to get to the base of the stone. She reaches for the handle of the sword, but as she grabs it, it disappears into thin air. Her jaw drops as she tries to comprehend what just happened. "But... what...?" she mumbles.

"Aria, are you okay?" Liam hurries over to her, increasingly worried.

"I promise... Liam... Excalibur..." Aria mumbles, unable to explain any further.

Arthur rolls his eyes to the sky. "You really aren't ready for this mission," he declares. "If you see imaginary things, we will not succeed."

Liam turns slowly to him, brows furrowed. "*You're* saying that?" he snaps. As he turns back to check on his friend, he spots something. He almost faints as he sees the same cute little birdhouse attached to the top of the tree trunk.

A look of fear crosses his face as he stares at the tree. He mutters, "Aria... Aria... Look at the birdhouse!"

A wave of disbelief flows over her as she stares at the tree ahead. It seems impossible that this is the same birdhouse as before. But it is.

So they've been walking in circles.

CHAPTER 8
THE SPYING CATS

L ancelot sits motionless in disbelief. His hand that holds the parchment shakes as his heart begins to race. He struggles to find the strength to open and read the paper, which contains the chance of a lifetime, something he has only dreamed of. To become King of England? He's sure he has the courage and skills for the challenge. After all, he is renowned as the bravest knight in the realm.

Nonetheless, he has heard rumors about another boy being destined to become king. Something to do with an old druid named Merlin. He sweeps this idea out of his brain to regain his confidence. Some knights enter the inn, greeting him from a distance, bringing him back to the present moment.

Why has the Circle of Druids chosen him? Is it pure luck, or do they believe he has the necessary qualities? It must be the latter, he thinks. Druids leave nothing to luck. Every action they take follows their faith, without exception.

After taking a deep breath, he finally unties the knot and gently unrolls the parchment, which is damp from his sweaty hands. Unfurling the map, he begins to study the symbols that will lead him to Excalibur. It will be more complex than he previously thought.

DISGUISED AS CATS, Tanglewood and Faewind creep up on a trio of children arguing near the base of a tree. However, there is no sign of the ancient druid Merlin to be seen or felt.

Faewind speaks to Tanglewood mentally.

"Do you think it's them?" she asks.

"I think so, but who are those two children with Arthur?" Tanglewood wrinkles his muzzle to get a better look. The tall, blond young man can only be Arthur. He has his mother's eyes and the same long face as his father. Tanglewood doesn't recognize the other two, whose clothes and attitude are more than a little peculiar.

"Is it possible that Merlin has called for reinforcements?" Faewind asks.

"It is quite possible. Let me remind you that time travel is one of his specialties. But I wonder why he would bring two children. They surely cannot match our powers!" Tanglewood exclaims, watching them jump around and shout, disrupting the peace of the woods.

"All those years in the forest must have made him lose his mind," Faewind suggests.

"Perhaps, but it was his choice to disobey us and betray the Circle. Now we have to make sure they never get to Excalibur," Tanglewood responds.

As they're about to set off again, an elderly man approaches the group, a cane clenched in his right hand to help him navigate the obstacles of the forest. His walk is as brisk as his legs will allow.

The eyes of the two felines widen. Seeing their childhood best friend after so long is far more emotional than they expected. Besides the deepened wrinkles on his face, Merlin hasn't changed much. He's still wearing his emerald druid robe, the same that they wear, and his long white hair reaches down to his buttocks. They watch in silence as the magician tries to calm the argument that has broken out among his group. Suddenly, he whirls around a tree before glaring at the thick mist covering their legs.

After remaining still for a long time, he finally glances up and meets the eyes of the two cats. They scurry away.

ARIA IS TRANSFIXED as a bird alights on the wooden house at the top of the tree. Liam stands behind her, watching too. Questions swirl in his mind as he wonders if he's losing his grasp on reality.

"What's the matter with you two?" Arthur asks, bewildered.

Aria points to the birdhouse and says, "We've seen this before! Actually, we've been here before!" She gestures around them.

Arthur bursts out laughing, to his companions' annoyance.

"We're going around in circles, and you're laughing!" Liam exclaims, stiffening.

"I'm laughing because you're losing your minds," Arthur retorts. "I knew the old man had lost some of his magical powers in recent years, but this time he's outdone himself. As well as finding Excalibur on my own, I will have to deal with two lunatics!"

Aria's flushes. "Because you're not a lunatic?" she retorts threateningly. "You've attacked an imaginary bear like a mad person, and you dare criticize us!" she continues, waving her index finger in Arthur's face.

"Well said, Aria!" Liam adds.

Arthur remains silent, clutching the scabbard of his dagger. Aria and Liam's indignation make him uneasy.

Everyone stares at each other, the silence between them growing more and more uncomfortable. Suddenly, Liam shouts "I know! It's Merlin's vigor elixir. That's what must be making us lose our minds!"

Arthur rolls his eyes "Of course not. I'm not delirious like you two!"

Aria ignores him, thinks for a moment, then responds, "Liam, I think you're right. Everything started after we drank it."

"Yes, I'm telling you, the old man tried to poison us," Liam shouts, grasping his head in his hands. "For all we know, their whole story might be fake, and it's a trap!"

Aria stares at him for a few seconds, realizing

that he has a point. Her history books don't mention any Arthur; only Lancelot is ever written about.

Arthur's face is strained and fearful. "Now tell us the truth!" Aria demands.

"What truth?" Arthur mumbles.

"Did Merlin try to poison us?" Liam advances menacingly on Arthur, who takes a step back.

"But if Merlin poisoned you, he did the same to me since I drank the same potion," the teenager points out, making Aria and Liam pause for thought. "He would never do something like that to me. I'm the most important thing in his world!"

Aria fixates on Arthur's eyes before declaring, "I think he's telling the truth, Liam."

"Maybe, but that doesn't explain what's happening to us," Liam objects.

Without warning, Merlin materializes, swaying from side to side until he joins the group.

"What is going on?" Merlin asks.

Liam rolls his eyes, pretending exasperation. "You need to tell us what's going on. We're going around in circles, and these two are turning delusional!"

Everything goes silent as Merlin looks around. He advances toward the tree with the birdhouse, walking around its enormous trunk. The golden filament that marks the way to the Circle of Druids' village still points north like it has since they set off on their quest.

Merlin rejoins the group, but his gaze lingers in the distance. Suddenly, he spots two black cats, but they swiftly fade into the fog. His stillness makes the others uneasy.

The druid ventures further into the forest, then drops to one knee and takes a deep whiff of the dense fog surrounding them. He stands back up and turns to face the others. "I sense magic. The Circle of Druids knows that we are looking for Excalibur. It is better to camp here before nightfall because we will not be able to avoid their traps in the dark," he declares.

"Excuse me, M-Merlin," Liam stutters. "But what do you mean by '*I sense magic*'? Because my dear comrade Aria and I didn't sign up for this."

The druid peers at him, making Liam even more uncomfortable. "This is not an ordinary fog," Merlin finally explains. "It's not damp and cold enough for such a mist at this time of day. It's a magical mist which will make you see many unreal things."

Liam chuckles loudly to mask his discomfort, but Aria stays quiet, focusing on the old druid.

"And you are right about going in a circle,"

Merlin adds as Liam suddenly stops laughing, overcome by fear. "We have barely travelled any distance since we started walking."

"But who's doing this to us?" Aria asks.

Merlin smiles faintly. "This, my child, is the work of my two oldest friends, Tanglewood and Faewind. I would recognize their magic among any," he declares, nodding toward the place where the cats had stood.

Aria and Liam gawk at each other, their minds spinning as they try to take all this in.

CHAPTER 9

THE DRUIDS' RIDDLES

L ancelot examines the parchment several times, his eyes narrowing as he tries to make sense of the confusing text. The druid previously spoke to him about a map that would lead him to Excalibur, but what is on this paper seems more like riddles. He shakes his head to clear it, then swigs some water to compose himself. He takes a moment before looking at the delicate hand-writing on the parchment again. He is hopeful that the text is a kind of map, a series of puzzles that will guide him toward Excalibur. Every passage conveys a clue.

Find thee the Oak, sturdy and old,
With limbs outstretched above the mold.
Seek its kin with a warrior's scar,
Struck by light from the sky afar.

When moon doth glow with argent light,
Three stones aligned will guide thee right.
Two twins stand, steadfast and bold,
The third in line, a secret it holds.

Seek the tranquil glade where azure waters lie,
A peaceful lake reflects the boundless sky.
In the clearing's heart, beneath the clay,
truths are revealed to those who find the way.

In a cavern deep, where shadows play,
A test of balance shall lead the way.
Sacrifice, not the life that blooms,
And Excalibur's rest will flee the glooms.

After reading the verses thoroughly twice, Lancelot pauses and looks ahead. If only the druids had *drawn* a map like everyone else! Now, he's embarking on a treasure hunt with an enormous prize awaiting him at the end. Carefully, he studies the opening verse again. The oak must be the first stop in his quest. After rereading the parchment one last time, he rolls it up and hides it in his satchel.

There's no time to spare. Someone else might be hunting for Excalibur already. He can't afford to miss this opportunity. Lancelot bolts out of the door without saying a word to his fellow knights in the inn, determined to find Excalibur alone.

STILL DISGUISED AS CATS, Tanglewood and Faewind race through the forest. The sun is dipping below the horizon, but their excellent eyesight gives them an edge at night. After discovering a hollow in a nearby tree, the two druids climb inside it to rest.

"Do you think he saw us?" Faewind asks. Her fur is damp from the foggy air.

Tanglewood shakes his head. "No, I don't think so. He would have come after us. However, it looks like he found out we cast a spell. We must come up with something a bit cleverer if we want to keep them away."

"But how can we do that?" Faewind asks. "If Merlin realizes what we have done, he will protect himself with a magical bubble like before, and our magic will be ineffective!"

Tanglewood stays quiet for a while. This possibility is very likely. "We must figure out who the two children with them are and what their purpose is here."

They leave the hollow tree at once and return to the Circle of Druids. But they will have to wait until everyone is asleep before they can act.

MERLIN STEPS AWAY from the group and taps the earth with his cane. He stands between three medium-sized trees, whose roots barely protrude from the soil. He strikes the ground repeatedly until the hovering mist dissipates into the undergrowth.

Liam runs to catch up with the druid, trailed by Aria. "Hold on—who are Tanglewood and Faewind? I listened carefully in class," Liam declares, though Aria looks disbelieving, "but no one ever speaks about these two," he protests, waving his arms.

"I'm sad to say it, but Liam is right. We don't know them," Aria agrees.

Merlin, who has remained calm, lowers himself to the ground and takes a handful of soil in his hands. He brings it up to his nose and inhales, for no obvious reason. After dropping the soil again, he raises his index finger and closes his eyes.

"What on earth is he doing?" Liam asks Aria.

"It must be a Druid thing! I read they're really connected to nature," Aria says.

Merlin remains silent but slowly rises to his feet, pushing up the sleeves of his robe. He closes his eyes and takes a deep breath. A gentle smile spreads across his face as he opens his arms. With a powerful thrust, he stabs his cane into the ground. At the second strike, cracks open in the earth at the feet of the two adventurers. They step back as the three trees around them magically move apart, making a big open space.

Merlin approaches Aria and Liam in silence, stopping outside the newly created space. He snaps the fingers of his left hand, and particles of gold dust spin outward from his grasp to form a tornado. Aria and Liam squint in bewilderment at the brilliant whirlwind swirling around them. When the golden dust settles, a camp made up of four bedrolls surrounding a crackling bonfire appears before their eyes.

Arthur, who has been sitting on a tree trunk, jumps off to head for the campfire. Merlin joins him soon after, strolling past Aria and Liam, who remain perfectly still.

"Are you going to stay there all night, or will you come and join us?" Arthur asks.

Aria shakes her head, trying to wake herself up. But she is finally realizing that this is not a dream, at least not in the literal sense. Ever since she was a child, she's wondered if magic exists. History is full of unbelievable feats that could surely not have been achieved without the power of magic. As the reality of what she's seeing finally sinks in, she skips back to the campsite, her face glowing with enthusiasm, forgetting about all their past misadventures.

"Liam!" she calls as she takes a seat between Merlin and Arthur.

Liam remains standing there, stunned. Merlin has already done some unbelievable things just by snapping his fingers. But moving trees? Making a camp appear? It's too much for his scientific mind to digest.

But the sound of laughter from the others as they settle around campfire starts to draw him back into reality. With utmost caution, he takes one slow step after another toward the campfire.

"I see you've finally wised up, my dear Liam," Aria teases. "Good for you, because the food is delicious!"

Liam's eyes widen with surprise. What did she just say? Aria doesn't usually like food at all! Were they enchanted after all? He sits on the last available straw mat and hesitantly accepts the chicken skewer Arthur offers him. He gingerly brings the food up to his nose for a sniff, wondering what might be wrong with it.

"Why are you sniffing like that?' Aria demands when she notices what he is doing. "You love chicken!" Merlin and Arthur look at Liam too, embarrassing him even more.

Does she always have to put them in this type of situation? "No, no, nothing…" he stammers before taking a bite.

"Merlin," Aria begins, "I'd like to understand something. Who are…" She pauses as she tries to remember their names.

"Tanglewood and Faewind!" Liam chimes in, through a mouthful of chicken.

Merlin smiles at them before sighing. "Tanglewood and Faewind were my best friends growing up. We were an unstoppable trio," he explains, unable to suppress a smile as he remembers those times. "Today, they are considered the most powerful druids in the Circle. Even though I have more skill than them, there was no way I could defeat them when they joined forces against me."

"Joined forces against you?" Liam's voice is garbled, his mouth full of food.

"Yes, you see, when they discovered Arthur's presence, they united against us," Merlin explains, a tear rolling down his cheek.

Aria and Liam exchange a worried glance, wondering if something like that could happen to them, the best friends in the world. "You mean, they are the ones from the Circle of Druids who decided to go against you?" Aria asks.

"Exactly," Merlin confirms. "They convinced the other council members to come after Arthur and me."

"What did they do exactly?" Liam asks.

Seeing his adoptive father on the verge of breaking down, Arthur answers, "They tried to kidnap me."

Aria and Liam nearly choke on their food when they hear what Merlin's best friends have done.

CHAPTER 10

THE GRAND OAK TREE

Merlin recounts the troubling stories of Tanglewood and Faewind's actions. They attempted to weaken his magic and spread false tales among the Circle of Druids, making them believe Merlin was endangering England without care. To top it off, they even hatched a plan to kidnap young Arthur.

Liam's eyes bulge with incredulity. "Unbelievable," he mutters.

Merlin nods. "That's why I had to form a protective circle to shield us from being found. But now that we have left it, our presence has been detected, and they will go to any lengths to hinder our progress."

Aria asks, "What makes you sure they know we're here?"

"Did you see that heavy fog that we were caught up in before?" Merlin asks. "And now it's no longer here?"

"Yes!" the three reply in unison.

"Well, that's the Mist of Illusion. It creates visions to confuse travelers."

Aria and Liam both let out a long breath as they realize the cause of their scary madness. "That's why he saw a bear!" Liam exclaims. Arthur raises his eyebrows, still convinced he fended off a terrifying beast.

"The bear was really there, and I must say I outdid myself fighting it!" Arthur retorts, puffing out his chest.

Aria and Liam grit their teeth, but don't bother arguing with him.

"And when I saw Excalibur, it wasn't really there," Aria adds, her eyes suddenly gleaming with excitement as she realizes she's been a victim of a real magical spell.

"Yes, exactly!" Merlin confirms. "They're trying to confuse us. They're doing it with the path too. That's why you saw the exact same birdhouse. They probably cast a spell so that the golden filament would create a loop of sorts."

"But if that's the case, how will we find the village?" Aria asks, glancing at the filament still floating in the air.

"We'll have to be ingenious, I suppose," Merlin replies.

"You two have work to do!" Arthur declares loudly.

"If you want to escape this maze, you'd better help us! Not to mention that these druids are after you, not us!" Liam retorts with a glare, pointing at Arthur.

Merlin snaps his fingers and instantly puts out the flame, startling everyone. This is not the time for another argument. The sun set quite a while ago. They must rest so as to be at their best tomorrow.

Besides, night is a time for reflection.

STILL DISGUISED AS CATS, Tanglewood and Faewind creep up to the camp. Although it's almost dark, they easily spot the group around the campfire from afar, nibbling chicken on skewers. Their sensitive feline noses pick up the delightful aroma. Merlin must have sensed their magic as the Mist of Illusion they had created is gone.

As soon as Merlin extinguishes the bonfire, the tranquility of the forest returns. Hiding amid tangled ivy, the cats remain motionless as owls hoot in the distance.

As the hours pass, they remain wide awake. From their vantage point, they observe the camp where the entire group is sleeping soundly. Tanglewood's nose wrinkles as he picks up a scent that Faewind cannot detect; he turns his head toward her and says, "I think we can get closer."

Faewind gives a nod of acknowledgment before rising to her feet. Tanglewood walks ahead slowly, taking care not to step on the crisp leaves and make a noise. His partner follows him, exercising just as much vigilance.

When they are just a few feet from the campsite, an abrupt, gruff noise breaks the peace. Tanglewood jumps up in surprise before flattening himself on the ground to hide. The threatening noise sounds a second time.

The younger boy stands up and yells, "Aria! Can't you stop snoring? You're keeping me awake!"

The girl's only response is a quiet whistling sound—another snore.

Tanglewood and Faewind watch from a discreet distance, their furry bodies pressed against the ground to avoid detection. They remain like this until they hear the boy breathe heavily. With the sun soon to rise, they have no time to waste!

"Let's split up," Tanglewood suggests to Faewind before heading toward the camp. "You can take the girl, and I'll take the boy."

Tanglewood is now at Liam's feet, sniffing him carefully. Faewind does the same with Aria, who is lying beside the smoldering fire. Suddenly, a loud, deep sound escapes from Aria's open mouth: more snoring. Faewind takes a few steps back and glances at Tanglewood, who is still carefully sniffing at Liam's face.

Liam opens his eyes, preparing to yell at Aria again. Instead, when he sees Tanglewood's wrinkled snout in front of him, he lets out a bloodcurdling scream.

Tanglewood cat's eyes bulge as he emits a loud meow before fleeing back to the woods. Faewind narrowly avoids landing in his lap when he stands up as she hops over him.

Aria jolts awake and cries out in panic, "What's happening?"

Despite his age, Merlin jumps to his feet and

gazes at the woods. He watches the cats dash away until he can no longer see them.

"Cat! On me!" Liam mumbles, disoriented.

"What?" Aria exclaims, incredulous.

Arthur is fast asleep, unaware of the chaos around him. Liam stands up, his face pale and his legs trembling. Merlin swiftly approaches and says, "You have just met Tanglewood and Faewind." His eyes dart in the direction of the two cats who just escaped.

Aria and Liam are struck speechless, utterly stunned by this nocturnal meeting with the most dangerous of the druids.

LANCELOT HAS ALREADY BEEN WALKING for a few hours. Yet he has not seen any sign of the grand old oak mentioned on the druids' map. He stops for a moment and wipes away the sweat dripping down his forehead. How will he ever find one specific oak tree in an entire forest when so many stand?

The riddle suggests that it has been struck by lightning. Could this give him a clue to its location? Suddenly, he hears footsteps approaching him. Two young women come into view, carrying baskets brimming with leaves. He quickly tucks the parchment away in his satchel.

He squints at the leaves before him to identify them. They are greener than usual for the season, with about five deep smooth-edged lobes on each leaf. His eyes light up; these are oak leaves!

The two young women approach him, smiling. "Do you need help?" one asks in a soft voice.

Lancelot gazes into her eyes, and she gazes back. "No, thank you," he answers abruptly, picking up his bag and continuing on his path. Lancelot resumes his own course, following the prints left by the young women on the muddy ground. When he turns around one last time to see if they've gone, they are still there, watching him with a hint of mischief in their eyes. He quickly turns his head back around and increases his pace, fearing someone might discover his true mission in the forest.

After several minutes of proceeding at a steady jog, he spots a small clearing in the distance. He stops and kneels to study some tracks on the ground. The footprints are the same shape as those made by the young women's boots earlier. Suddenly filled with fresh hope, he runs toward the clearing.

He pushes the branches of a bush aside, and at last, his eyes fall upon a grand old oak, which stands majestically in the middle of the clearing, its long limbs like outstretched arms beckoning to the gentle wind. Its powerful roots snake through the ground below, forming secret maps on the floor. Every leaf seems lit by its own light, and tiny magical acorns litter the earth around the trunk.

Lancelot approaches the tree cautiously, mesmerized by its beauty and might. He circles it, taking in all of its features. Suddenly, he notices a jagged crack snaking from the roots to the very top of the trunk—likely caused by a bolt of lightning.

He jumps up in celebration, restraining himself from yelling out loud. He has succeeded in the first step without any help.

Before long, he will be King of England!

CHAPTER II

THE SECRET
CONVERSATION

M erlin slowly moves closer to the slumbering Arthur, extending an arm to softly nudge his shoulder. The teenager mutters unintelligible noises, his eyes remaining firmly closed. Aria and Liam, now recovered from the shock of their strange meeting with Faewind and Tanglewood, are starting to grow impatient. Unable to wait anymore, Aria strides over to a bucket of water next to the recently doused fire. She lifts it and carries it toward Merlin, who is still being far too gentle in his attempts to wake Arthur. "Wait, I've got this! I have experience," Aria exclaims, lifting the bucket with both hands. "Step back, Merlin!"

Liam giggles; he knows from long experience

how unpleasant it is to be so harshly awoken. Aria swings the bucket backward to gain momentum before tossing its contents at the teenager's head. The moment the water touches Arthur's skin, he jerks awake and leaps up.

"What are you thinking? Are you trying to give him a cold?" Merlin protests to Aria, rushing over to Arthur, who is dripping wet.

"Have you lost your mind?" Arthur yells, quickly getting up and shoving Merlin in the process. He begins to jump up and down in an attempt to shake off the water.

Liam's face lights up with delight as he exclaims, "You gave us no other choice! We yelled and shouted, but you wouldn't wake up. You could have been attacked and you'd have slept through it!"

"Yeah, and besides, you're not made of sugar. You'll recover," Aria adds with a smirk. "If you need advice, ask Liam. He's used to it."

Arthur is speechless.

"Alright, that's enough," Liam says as he scans the area. "We've got a village to find, and some murderous druids —so we don't have time to waste."

"*Murderous?*" Arthur is alarmed.

"You would know if you hadn't slept like a

rock," Aria twits him before inspecting the muddy ground.

Merlin assists Arthur with wringing out his damp cloak, taking advantage of the moment to fill him in on what has happened this morning.

Aria, half-bent over, furrows her brows as she spots something on the ground. Liam stares at her. "What are you doing?" he asks. She remains half-crouched as she takes another step forward.

"See?" she says, gesturing to the wet earth. Liam comes closer and kneels down to take a better look. "There are pawprints here. I bet Tanglewood and Faewind went this way."

Liam gazes at her, puzzled. "What does that have to do with our mission?"

Aria quickly straightens up and puts her hands on her hips. "Oh, come on, Liam! With any luck, there will be traces along their route, and that will lead us to the village!"

Aria continues following the trail of footsteps when Liam suddenly suggests, "Why not follow the filament instead?" At that, she halts in her tracks and stands up straight. Her gaze lingers on the thin golden filament that has guided them since their journey started. She smiles widely as she turns around to face Liam, catching him off guard.

"Liam, this is the filament making us go in a circle," she sighs. "Like Merlin told us, they must have put a spell on it, because the pawprints don't go in the same direction as the filament! You would know if you hadn't been so busy eating chicken!"

"Very well, Sherlock Holmes," Liam challenges her, "but who's to say they didn't go somewhere else?"

"Why wouldn't they?" Aria argues. "It's possible, but I don't think that's what happened, seeing as they've been rumbled. Better for them to return to the village where they're safe."

Merlin and Arthur come hurrying over. Arthur still looks annoyed.

Seeing Aria and Liam in the middle of an intense discussion, Merlin asks what's going on. Aria fills him in, and he studies the tracks carefully before breaking into a delighted grin. "I believe you are right. Let's follow them!" he declares.

"Fantastic, let's get going! We've wasted enough time as it is," Aria cries as she hurries along beside the pawprints, her seemingly inexhaustible energy still intact although she has drunk no potion.

THE FOUR OF them march through the forest in silence. Merlin takes his time at the back of the group due to his achy legs. Arthur walks ahead with a sour expression on his face, and Aria has her eyes fixed on the path of footprints. Liam follows her closely.

"Psst, Aria!" Liam calls to her in a low voice.

"What do you want?" she responds, still not lifting her gaze from the trail.

Liam quickly catches up with her, knowing she won't slow down.

"Do you think we can trust them? I hope it's not a trap," he whispers.

Aria abruptly raises her head while continuing to walk. "Why do you say that?"

"I don't know. I just have a bad feeling about them. Merlin didn't seem too upset to see Tangle-wood and Faewind in the camp," he explains, shaking his head slightly.

Aria's face scrunches up as she reflects in silence. "Yes, but what can we do? Merlin brought us here; if we fail, we will not be able to return to Sommetville. And let's not forget what these druids have done to Merlin! I think we should be more careful of Arthur; he doesn't seem so happy with us."

Liam turns to observe the teenager. Arthur is

wearing a stern expression as he attempts to rub some warmth into his arms. "At any rate, he didn't appreciate your wake-up method, my dear Aria!" Liam chuckles.

"What can I say, my dear Liam? Not everyone has your courage." She smiles before redirecting her attention to the tracks.

As they reach a small clearing with a single, large tree standing in the middle, Aria raises her eyes.

Liam lets out an impressed "Wow!" as he circles the great trunk. Aria gazes up at its highest branches, her eyes filled with admiration. Arthur arrives soon after, not quite grasping what all the excitement is about—it's just a tree, after all!

When Merlin appears, he beams at Aria and Liam. Since his youth, the druid has been taught the immense significance trees hold on earth. "This is an ancient oak," Merlin exclaims. "These are sacred trees and very important for us druids."

"Look! There's a crack in its trunk!" Liam exclaims. Aria races to get a better look.

Arthur, however, hangs back. "Yes, very nice, but we should get going. No time to waste on a tree even older than Merlin!" He strides forward without turning back. Aria and Liam frown: he's becoming insufferable.

"If we find Excalibur, maybe it should be us who pulls it from the stone," Liam whispers to Aria.

"You could, my dear Liam. You'd make a good king, you know," Aria agrees. "But then you'd have to forget all your tech and soccer games! Not to mention the amusement park, camping, and our wild adventures. You'll be too busy reigning!"

Reluctantly, Liam admits she has a point and resumes his journey.

A short walk later, they arrive at the outskirts of a tranquil village. Quickly, they hide behind some nearby foliage; the large green leaves make for great cover. Finally, Merlin joins them, overwhelmed with emotion as he lays eyes upon his hometown for the first time in years.

People of all ages, wearing long robes in varying emerald green and sapphire blue hues with geometric symbols stitched in gold, wander around or converse in small groups. Suddenly, Merlin's pulse quickens. At the far end of the central space, he spots a couple about his age, dressed in matching emerald robes, walking toward them. A young man in a sweeping blue robe comes into view to meet them.

He gestures to Aria, Liam, and Arthur and whispers, "That's Tanglewood and Faewind! Let's go hide there so we can hear them." Merlin tiptoes hunched over toward a line of shrubbery that borders the town. The other three stay close behind him, keeping themselves low to avoid detection. They are near enough to hear the druids' conversation.

"So?" Tanglewood asks.

"Lancelot has already managed to pass the first two stages," the man exclaims, his voice labored from the effort of running. The two druids break into smiles.

"Excellent. That means it won't be long before he finds Excalibur!" Faewind declares.

Aria and Liam listen in dismay. How are they going to outmaneuver Lancelot and find Excalibur first?

CHAPTER 12

BRANCHBOUNCEFLYERS

ancelot hurries along a winding path in the woods, prickly shrubs painfully scratching his face. Sweaty and bloodied, he stops to catch his breath. After locating the oak tree, it didn't take long for him to find the three oval stones. Many pathways lead into the clearing, but he's found the right one on only his second try.

A few feet away from the oak tree clearing, in a path bordered by bushes and trees, stands the oval stones arranged in a line. The map mentions the moon, but he can't gamble on waiting for nightfall with time running out.

Sitting in front of the last stone, he sees an arrow pointing to a path. He takes out the map once more to reread the next clue.

Seek the tranquil glade where azure waters lie,
A peaceful lake reflects the boundless sky.
In the clearing's heart, beneath the clay,
truths are revealed to those who find the way.

The arrow on the stone must indicate the path to a lake. He stands up and spots two horses grazing on the grass not far from him. One notices him and comes closer as if to ask if he needs help. Lancelot pauses for a long time before eventually walking away. He knows he can rely only on himself for this mission, so he walks instead of riding. This way, he won't be at the mercy of an unpredictable animal.

The path is long and arduous; after several hours of trudging along, there is still no view of the lake. As his energy starts to dwindle, he decides it's time to take a break. The urge to sleep is strong; he hasn't rested since he set out on his mission. But slumber is not an option as the stakes are too high. Who knows how many people the druids have given the map to? He hasn't encountered anyone else yet, but letting his guard down so close to the goal is out of the question.

As THE DRUIDS finish their conversation, they all go their separate ways. Tanglewood and Faewind walk toward the council room while the other man heads toward a nearby house. Merlin watches them, a mixture of emotions stirring in his heart. Seeing them again brings back so many memories—but he knows they want Lancelot to be crowned king.

Aria, Liam, and Arthur remain still, scared of being found out. This is the first time Arthur has been so quiet since their journey began, and his usually arrogant expression has turned sad. He covers his nose and mouth to muffle his tears.

Arthur rises to his feet and scurries behind a thick tree trunk. Liam taps Aria's shoulder to indicate they should follow him. As they meet him, Arthur is crying, his head buried in his hands. Liam and Aria wonder what to do. Arthur's attitude is vile, but he's obviously in pain.

Aria approaches him and gently places her hand on his shoulder, "Don't worry, Arthur, we will find Excalibur," she reassures him.

"Let's not make any promises we can't keep," Liam says in a low voice to Aria. At this, Arthur looks up.

"It's all my fault!" Arthur proclaims between sobs. "I thought being king was my destiny and it would all happen without me making any effort. I wasted time doing nothing, and now I… I could lose everything!" he splutters, wiping his tears with his cloak. Aria and Liam exchange fleeting glances. They didn't anticipate something like this.

"It's true, you're right," Liam begins. "But all is not lost. Aria and I can help you, but you'll have to put in the effort because it's your destiny, not ours!"

Liam's challenge sparks a slight smile from Arthur.

"Thank you… I'm sorry for treating you that way… I've been so used to getting everything I want from Merlin that I thought it would happen again…" Arthur mumbles.

"Don't worry, I know what it's like," Aria sympathizes.

"That's for sure!" Liam chimes in, earning himself a sharp glare.

Eventually, Merlin joins them. Arthur turns to him, smiling awkwardly. "Merlin," he starts, "how can we find the map? How can we get it back if it was given to Lancelot?"

Merlin looks amused. "Surely you don't believe there's only one! Every map, paper, and document created by the Circle of Druids is kept carefully in the archive house, which you see over there." He points to a building at the edge of the forest a few feet away.

"So, you mean there's definitely a copy of the map?" Aria checks.

"Yes! All you have to do is go and get it," Merlin assures her.

"Great, I'm off!" Arthur declares before dashing away, Liam close at his heels.

"Hold on a minute!" Liam says, grabbing Arthur's sleeve. "I'm glad you've found your motivation, but we won't let you go alone. We're stronger together, remember? Plus, we won't have time to search the entire house. So, we need a specific plan!"

"Well said, my dear Liam!" Aria agrees.

"I'll use my magic to make the map sparkle," Merlin suggests eagerly.

"Won't that give away your location?" Aria asks.

"I don't think so, but at worst, they'll capture me, and you will continue your mission! Finding Excalibur is more important," the old druid responds.

"Merlin…" Arthur begins, but Liam quickly jumps in, guessing what Arthur is about to say.

"Every big adventure means giving up something," Liam says. "If Merlin's okay with it, we should be too." Focusing his attention on the house,

Liam adds, "Let's see how we can get into this place."

Aria moves closer to Liam, studying the house. Then she jumps with excitement. "I know, I know!" The others shush her, but she keeps going as if she hasn't heard them. Eventually, she covers her mouth with both hands to muffle her enthusiasm.

Liam asks quietly, "What is it?"

"Look at the tree above the house. It's almost the same as the one from the BranchBounceFlyers course!" she tells him with a huge smile.

"Not bad!" responds Liam, catching on at once. "This is a chance for some bonus practice!" He clasps his hands together and then extends them in front of him to warm up.

"I thought we didn't need training?" Aria retorts with a sly smile.

"Not me, but you do! You're way too clumsy, and it's costing us points!" Liam reproaches her.

"What?" Aria exclaims in shock before muttering, "I may be clumsy, but you always think you can reach two branches above, and in the end, it loses us time!"

Merlin and Arthur look from Liam to Aria and back, trying to understand what they're talking about.

Arthur finally raises his finger between them before asking, "Sorry, but what is the Branch-Bounce... er..."

"Flyers!" Aria and Liam finish in unison.

"It's a mega-popular sport where we live," Liam explains.

"It's super simple," Aria interjects. "It's tree acrobatics! You got to leap from branch to branch. There might be a few obstacles on the way. Every successful leap will score you a point!"

When Merlin and Arthur still look blank, Liam elaborates, "The most important thing to remember is that we're trained in tree acrobatics, so it'll be easy for us to reach the branch above the house."

"But what do we do when we get up there?" Aria frets, gesturing toward the rooftop. "We can't just jump down on the house or enter through the door—someone might see us!"

Liam agrees and points out that even though the house is set back from the path, there's a danger of being seen.

"I know!" Arthur turns to the druid and asks, "Merlin, do you think you could create a window in the roof like you did in my bedroom?"

"You're a genius!" Merlin exclaims, and plants a huge kiss on the cheek of his adoptive son. "And don't worry about the inside! The archive room is always empty." He rolls up his sleeves, ready to get to work.

Aria, Liam, and Arthur slowly walk to the tree beside the archive house. Liam takes the lead, firmly gripping the tree trunk and scaling it as effortlessly as a chimpanzee until he reaches the first branch. He grabs onto a low limb and swings his right leg over the top of it before standing up. Agile and confident, he strides toward the branch closest to the house.

Aria opts for a more acrobatic approach. She runs full speed at the tree and leaps up the trunk, wrapping her arms around it to support herself. But as she swings her legs up to one of the branches, her excitement makes her lose her balance and sends her spinning around it. Liam, who is preparing to bounce two branches at once so as to move faster, sends her an accusing look when he sees her spinning.

Arthur watches them from below, marveling at their strength and agility. He has seriously underestimated them. At last, he takes a deep breath and plucks up the courage to follow. His palms are already slick with sweat by the time he's halfway up the tree and reaches the first branch with some difficulty. Arthur watches from below as Aria performs a graceful balancing act before jumping onto the next branch with perfect precision.

Liam has finally reached the branch above the house when he spots a chipmunk heading directly toward him. He screams in fear, making Aria wobble and almost lose her balance. She throws herself flat against the branch in an attempt to hide. Liam's screams have attracted the attention of some nearby druids, who start looking around.

CHAPTER 13

THE ARCHIVE HOUSE

Arthur stands completely still, hand clasped around a tree branch, the earthy-brown hues of his cloak enabling him to blend into the bark. He hardly dares move his head to check on Aria and Liam. Eventually, he makes out a barely audible noise coming from somewhere nearby.

Aria quietly creeps along the tree branch to come up behind Liam. She makes a soft hissing sound to get Arthur's attention. He turns around and sees her motioning for him to join them.

He takes a deep breath before mustering the courage to move toward them like a tightrope walker. Several branches separate him from the adventurers, who are starting to get impatient as they watch him progress at a snail's pace. He climbs carefully, reaching out to grasp higher branches for balance as he puts one foot in front of the other. He looks down below him before quickly lifting his head. He didn't know he had a fear of heights—but now it overwhelms him. Ignoring the glares of his companions, he takes his time to advance.

Once Arthur is finally standing at the back of the line, Liam gets on with the next part of the plan.

"That was close, but they didn't see us!" he whispers, focusing on the roof of the archive house, waiting for the window to appear.

"If you hadn't lost your nerve at the sight of a chipmunk, we'd already have the map!" Aria snaps back impatiently.

"Merlin hasn't even created the window yet!" Liam exclaims, pointing to the thatched roof. "And besides, do we really believe he can?"

"Don't worry, I've seen him do it," Arthur assures them. "We just have to be patient."

Aria sighs before sitting up, one leg dangling on each side of the branch. Patience is not her strong suit.

Everyone holds their breath as they eagerly await the appearance of the window that will finally give them access to the map.

LANCELOT SETTLES on a rock nestled between two prickly bushes at the bottom of the path and takes a loaf of bread from his satchel. He carefully avoids the thorns as he enjoys his meal. Then, his belly full, he wonders how far it is to the lake.

Fortunately, he hasn't encountered anyone yet, which is a good sign. Or did he take the wrong path? The thought makes his heart race. But he decides that's impossible and regains his composure. The sun is so high in the sky that its rays burn his face. When he goes to take another bite of his bread, he nearly misses. He's finding it more challenging to see, his eyelids drooping. Soon, it becomes impossible to fight the fatigue that overwhelms him. His eyes close, and he can no longer resist the pull of sleep. He slumps and tumbles into a deep slumber amidst the leaves of a tall bush. Only the sounds of his snores reach the trail.

HIDDEN at the top of the tree, the adventurers have been staying still for what feels like an eternity. Arthur sits behind Aria, his hands clamped firmly around the branch. He tries to stay calm, but the nausea from the height begins to blur his vision. Aria swings her legs in the air to cope with her hyperactivity, which is increased by boredom. Liam, for his part, has his eyes fixed on the roof, quite glad not to be behind Aria since her fidgeting always makes him lightheaded.

"There! It's coming!" Liam springs to life. Aria nearly topples him off the branch as she leans over to get a better view. Her face lights up as she observes golden dust tracing the shape of a skylight. "Wow!" she whispers, grinning.

As the golden dust evaporates, leaving a window in its place, Liam straightens up to adopt the same posture as the others. "Alright, I'll go first," he declares in a serious tone. "I'm going to open the skylight, and you guys can follow me afterward, okay?"

Aria winces as she looks at the skylight. Liam notices her and asks, "What is it?"

"Are you sure your weight won't break the roof when you jump?" she asks, her jaw tense. "Or at least make a loud noise?"

"Of course not!" Liam protests.

"She has a point," Arthur interjects.

Liam looks at the skylight again as his friends'

faces fill with determination. The length of the fall between the tree branch and the roof would indeed give him enough speed to make a not-so-graceful landing. However, they don't have any other options.

"I have a better idea!" Aria's sudden exclamation startles the other two. "Liam, you hang from the branch, and I'll climb down to you. That way, it'll be a shorter distance to jump down onto the roof." She beams at her friends as she explains her plan. "Then, I can open the skylight, and you guys can jump through!"

"You're completely insane!" Liam snaps, his face tense. "Why don't *you* hang from the branch while I come down?"

"Because you're bigger and stronger, my dear Liam. If we do it the other way around, I can promise we'll both end up with a broken leg!"

Liam bites his lip, knowing she's right. "What if we jump through the skylight and land on something sharp?" Liam says, and Arthur nods in agreement.

Aria's tone is challenging as she asks, "But Liam, do you really think I'm not going to check what's in there before you jump? Let's go! We don't have any time to waste!"

Liam hesitates for a moment before wrapping his hands around the branch like a gymnastics bar and throwing his left leg over it. He dangles from the branch, his legs swinging in the air. Aria begins to spin her arms and bend her beck, turning her head in circles at the same time.

"A-rrr-ii-aa," Liam whispers through clenched teeth. "Can you move faster? I'm not going to last long!"

"Yes! I'm coming. I was warming up!" she replies before shuffling forward onto her buttocks, closer to Liam's now reddened hands. With a precise movement, she stretches her arms over her teammate before bending them to slide against him. As she embraces his torso to descend, her weight nearly drags his hands off the branch.

"Hurry up, please!" Liam pleads, sweating.

Aria swarms down his body until her feet are just inches from the roof. She clenches her teeth as she is just atop the window. She begins to move her legs in a swing movement to take momentum. When she finds herself away from the window, she lets go of her grip and lands safely. Turning over to the skylight, she quickly opens it and peers inside to look for any sign of people. Below the window sits a wooden table with several documents spread out on top of it.

Jumping to her feet, she looks up at her friends in

alarm. "Be careful—" she starts to say before Liam suddenly loses his grip on the branch and slips through the skylight with a terrified shriek. Aria grimaces and leans over to see Liam spread-eagled on the table. "—there's a table," she finishes through gritted teeth.

Liam groans with pain, then replies, "Thanks, I know!"

"At least you won't fall any further!" she tells him, but before she can say any more, there's a loud crack. Liam's bodyweight is too much for the four table legs to handle, and they buckle under the pressure. He slides to the floor, crying out in pain as he lands.

Aria tries to encourage him by saying, "Thanks for taking one for the team and clearing a path for Arthur. Now, move aside so he can make his jump!" But her attempt at cheering Liam up only earns her an icy glare.

Nevertheless, he rolls to the side to make space. Despite his unease, Arthur boldly scrambles through the skylight, and Aria soon follows him. She chooses a more controlled method of descent, holding her arms over the sides of the window to slow herself down.

"You, okay?" Arthur asks Liam, extending a hand to help him up.

"Yes… thank you…" he mutters, wincing.

"Wow, you made quite a mess!" Aria teases. Liam and Arthur just stare her down. "I'm grateful we didn't follow your original plan, that's all," she continues with a hint of a smile. "Or else it would have been a nasty fall."

Liam doesn't acknowledge her words, scanning the room instead. The house has two narrow windows on either side of the front door and one more at the back, looking out onto the woods. When Liam sees it, he rolls his eyes in annoyance. If only they'd seen it, he would have been spared a big misadventure.

The walls are lined with shelves, bearing thousands of scrolls and reaching all the way up to the ceiling. As the group looks around, no light is coming from any scrolls. Then they start to wonder, what is Merlin doing?

CHAPTER 14
THE MAGICAL LIGHT

Merlin had struggled to create the skylight, distracted by the tumult of emotions he felt at returning to the village where he had lived for so long.

Hidden in his secret spot, he cringes and grimaces when he sees Liam plummet through the skylight. That landing must have hurt.

Now that the children have entered the archive house, he must start his second spell. He readjusts his druid robes, pushing the sleeves up to his elbows. Allowing his muscles to relax, he closes his eyes and holds out both hands in preparation for his spellcasting. Several seconds pass, and they remain still, unable to act on the commands from his mind. He is too nervous and distracted for the magic to work.

He opens his eyes again to refocus, his arms trembling as fear of failure washes through him. "You can do this, Merlin. You are a skilled druid!" he whispers to himself encouragingly. But despite his attempt to reassure himself, nothing happens. On the brink of despair, he looks around to see if an element of nature can help him regain his magic. He notices a group of children in their druid robes approaching the forest from the village square. He hides behind a tree while continuing to watch them.

They wear the same outfit that he and his two friends, Tanglewood and Faewind, wore when they attended the druid school. When he closes his eyes, he can feel the material on his skin: a hooded robe made of a blue as vivid as the sky with the emblem of an oak tree embroidered in golden threads. A smile forms as memories flood his mind.

His face lights up even more when he sees a young girl helping her friend levitate a green leaf from the ground. It makes him think about Faewind, who always encouraged him when they were children, helping him gain confidence in his abilities. Now, he remembers what she used to say when he was feeling down. "In the seeds of today's fear, find tomorrow's bloom, for the mightiest tree once feared its own room," he murmurs.

He looks toward the house and takes a deep breath. Closing his eyes, he snaps the fingers of his right hand. A brilliant beam of light shoots out of the skylight. Merlin's face beams, thrilled at his success. The light shines so brightly that he dims it with a slight movement of the head, not wanting to attract any attention.

Now, all he has to do is wait.

LIAM WANDERS THROUGH THE ROOM, squinting in hopes of catching a glimmer of light from a parchment. Arthur searches a shelf, lifting scrolls without knowing what he's looking for. At the same time, Aria heads toward a wall where stone tablets covered with symbols and writings are stored in a large tub. If someone had told her one day that she would find herself in a druid village, scouring their archives, she wouldn't have believed it. It's better than all the museums and history books she's ever visited or read!

She hesitates over a tablet that is engraved with verses, almost like poems, and drawings that remind her of her geometry classes. "Wow!" she exclaims.

"What? Did you find something?" Liam shouts, running toward her, quickly followed by Arthur.

Liam grimaces as he tries to decipher the message. "Man, this is worse than a puzzle! I would not like to have to decode something like this," he throws out sarcastically. "But try not to shout next time because you alerted us for nothing. This isn't the time for studying, my dear Aria!"

"Can't you just let me have this one moment?" Aria snaps before asking, "What do you think it is?"

Arthur pouts before responding, "In my opinion, it's a magical ritual! I recognize the symbols; Merlin has parchments filled with this kind of thing."

"We should try it," Aria suggests before meeting Liam's accusing gaze and subsiding.

"Help us look for this light instead..." Liam breaks off and shields his eyes with his arm as the tray begins to glow. His friends do the same in response as the light becomes blinding.

"The map! Grab it!" Liam yells at Aria, scrunching his face up to protect his eyes as much as possible.

"I can't. The light is blinding me!" Aria presses her arm to her eyes.

Arthur attempts to open his, but the white light burns his retinas. Suddenly, the light intensity diminishes. It takes Aria a few seconds to summon the courage to open one eye, which then takes a moment to adjust to the room's brightness. Once she's sure there's nothing amiss, she opens her other eye. One of the tablets in the tray is glimmering. She grabs one end of it with a single swift movement and quickly moves her other hand to support it from underneath. She hadn't expected the object to be so heavy.

The boys still have their eyes closed as she heads toward a central table. She shouts in victory, "I have it! I have it!"

Liam and Arthur finally open their eyes before joining Aria at the table. She is bent right over the tablet.

"What do you see?" Liam demands, trying to peer around her.

"Uh…" Aria stammers. "You're not going to like this!"

"What are you talking about? Let me see!" he implores. Aria moves aside to let him. Liam's expression turns from excited to disappointed. Engraved onto the tablet are four cryptic verses, coming together to form a riddle. Liam gives Arthur room to study it. "It's probably instructions for where to go—a map in verse," the teenager says.

"Thanks, we noticed!" Liam retorts. "Do you really think this is the right one? Maybe Merlin got his spell wrong."

"Will you stop blaming Merlin when things don't go the way you want?" Aria demands.

"Come on, Aria. Admit it! It doesn't really look like a map." Liam defends himself, gesturing toward the tablet.

"It is a map," Arthur intervenes. "It's very common for druids to create maps in riddles. It allows them to ensure that only someone really determined can find the location. I assure you, Merlin made me quite a few like this when I was a child. He said it would help me face life's trials!"

"It definitely worked," Liam can't help but say with sarcasm. To his great surprise, Arthur smiles in agreement.

"Okay, so you're used to deciphering them?" Aria asks.

Arthur swiftly reads the tablet. "I would say each verse corresponds to a step…" he murmurs. "An oak tree… stones…."

"Great, let's go before we're caught!" Aria suggests, looking around. "The window, over there! It opens on the forest."

"I know. I saw it as soon as I fell in," Liam grumbles.

"We couldn't have known; you can't see it from the outside." Aria grins before turning toward Arthur. "Arthur, take the tablet!"

The teenager tries, but his face reddens as his arms strain to lift the stone, now that the tabletop is no longer offering support.

"Not too heavy?" Liam asks, seeing Arthur walking with difficulty.

"No, no, don't worry…" Arthur stammers, his face getting redder. Liam races to help, and quickly understands the problem. Aria must have had an adrenaline rush to be able to carry the tablet so easily!

"We won't be able to do this," Liam exclaims as he strides back to the table with the tablet. "If we run, it'll take us too long. Let's just write down the instructions instead!"

Aria stops abruptly as she hears voices coming from outside. "We don't have time. Or anything to write with!" she exclaims. "Let's memorize a verse each," she suggests, hurriedly darting toward the tablet.

"No way! You'll mix up the lines with your talent

for jumbling words!" Liam responds. "If only we had a phone to take a picture!"

Aria's expression quickly brightens. "What is it now?" Liam asks, confused.

The girl starts to search the pockets of her hoodie. "Do you have your phone?" Liam asks hopefully, while Arthur looks on in confusion. "But we aren't allowed to have phones during competitions!"

Aria tugs open the zipper of her inner pocket, pulls out a phone and grins triumphantly at Liam. "Since when do I obey the rules? It's like you don't even know me!" She snaps a picture of the stone as Arthur stares, baffled by the strange device.

"My dear Aria, I've never appreciated your inability to follow the rules as much as now!" Liam rejoices.

"But... what is that?" Arthur stammers, frowning. "Are you magicians?" he asks while Aria and Liam exchange a look.

"We don't have time to explain now, but we promise we'll do it after we get out of here!" Liam promises before heading to the window.

Aria checks her photo. Seeing Arthur's bewilderment, she starts to show him the phone and explain how it works.

"Aria, now's not the time!" Liam shouts as he opens the small window.

"It's okay, I'm just showing him!" Aria defends herself.

While they are arguing, a door suddenly opens, and Aria and Arthur pivot to see who it is. Standing before them is the druid they saw with Tanglewood and Faewind. He looks both amazed and terrified to see them and raises his right hand to snap his fingers. Immediately, a loud siren, infused with an otherworldly magic, echoes throughout the village.

CHAPTER 15

THE INTRUDERS

A small squirrel is clambering through the bushes, collecting nuts in its cheeks. As the tiny creature moves quickly and silently through the thicket of lush green foliage, it suddenly spots a human lying on the ground. The man's face is peaceful, his eyes shut tight and his mouth slightly open. The squirrel edges closer, deciding to be kind and share the food it has collected.

Standing on its hind legs, the animal takes a nut from its overstuffed left cheek and places it in the man's open mouth.

The second the nut touches his tongue, Lancelot's jaw slams shut. His eyes shoot open as his brain registers the foreign object in his mouth. He is taken aback when he notices the tiny squirrel. One of its cheeks is stuffed with food, and it is gazing at him intently.

Lancelot jumps up and flings the animal away with a swipe of his arm, catapulting it toward the forest. The squirrel lands gracefully on a tree trunk, sinking its sharp claws into the bark. Then it scrambles up the tree until it reaches the topmost branch, where it settles down to enjoy its meal in peace.

Lancelot leaps to his feet, frantically scanning the forest for dangers. After composing himself, he realizes how foolish he was to doze off while eating. He looks up at the sky; the sun has passed its zenith. He must have slept for at least an hour!

Lancelot immediately resumes his run on the winding path. How could he have been so careless? He can only hope that the lake marked on the map is just a short distance away.

While he is still blaming himself for not being more careful, a flock of ten Little Egrets suddenly flies over him, brushing against his hair which is still tousled from his nap. He jumps and waves his arms to shoo them away—animals keep pestering him today! Then he realizes what this means: the lake must be nearby since Little Egrets are birds that live near water. He quickens his pace, striding purposefully; soon, he will find Excalibur.

ARIA, Liam, and Arthur all stand motionless, their legs turned toward the window. They hold their breath as they watch the druid standing in the door-way. The alarm is ear-piercing, and voices can be heard outside, drawing close.

Suddenly Aria shouts, "Go!" before throwing herself forward and leaping through the window. Liam barely manages to avoid her as she flies past. She lands on her front outside, her fall broken by bushes. The druid watches speechlessly as Liam leaps out of the window, opting to roll rather than dive.

"Arthur! Hurry up!" Liam yells back into the room. Aria is already standing up, ready to flee.

Arthur bolts to the window and dives, only to be caught as the man grabs hold of his cape at the last second. Arthur desperately kicks his legs to free himself from the druid's grip. Liam jumps up and takes hold of Arthur's arms, but he can't pull him through the window. With his body now horizontal, Arthur's panic increases when he looks over his shoulder and sees more druids sprinting outside toward the house.

Aria has spun around at the sound of a struggle

behind her. Now she darts back toward Liam to lend a hand. As other druids pile into the archive house, the two adventurers pull with all their might, and Arthur's cape rips.

"Thank you!" he gasps as he lands on his knees.

"Quick!" Aria shouts before running into the forest, closely followed by the others.

Liam says. "We need to find Merlin quickly!"

"He's never going to be able to run!" Arthur replies.

"It's a risk we'll have to take," Aria says, looking around for the elderly man.

Liam shouts a warning. "Look where you're going, or you'll trip over another root!"

"I got this!" Aria shouts as she weaves around a large trunk before suddenly crashing into an obstacle. She bounces backward and lands on her behind. Liam, who is right behind her, manages to jump over her in time, but he, too, is thrown off balance and collapses onto his knees.

"Merlin!" Liam exclaims. "Good timing, we were looking for you!"

Arthur arrives, and his face brightens with joy as he sees his adoptive father. He glances back and forth between Aria and Liam, perplexed by the sight of them lying on the ground.

Aria jumps up, adrenaline blocking out her pain. "We have to go! Now!" she orders.

Liam gets up too before looking at Merlin, "Can you run? They found us!"

"Of course, I can! When the alarm sounded, I thought I would never see you again!" Merlin sighs, tearing up. "Do you have the map?"

"Yes, though I wouldn't call it a map," Liam adds, raising his eyebrows.

"They're riddles!" Arthur explains.

"Oh! Riddles!" Merlin seems happy.

Aria looks behind her as she hears leaves rustling and twigs snapping. "Okay, I don't want to alarm you, but soon we'll have company. We better run!" she urges before opening her phone to look at the picture.

Liam snatches the phone. "What are you doing?" she cries.

"My dear Aria, let's not go over your clumsiness again. I'll take care of this," Liam responds, not breaking his stride as he accelerates.

Aria sighs in frustration before she follows him, paying attention to where she places her feet and what is in front of her—a sizeable challenge for her. Arthur takes Merlin's hand and leads him.

Liam tries his best to read the first verse. "The

oak tree! That's where we need to go!" he shouts, quickening the pace while trying to find his way through the undergrowth.

"Are you sure?" Aria calls out, following closely.

"He's right. I remember reading something like 'Find thee the Oak, sturdy and old... warrior's scar... struck by light...'" Arthur recalls snatches from memory.

"Yes! Aria, remember the huge scratch in the trunk!" Liam reminds her.

His heart pounding with excitement, Merlin yells, "The tree is on the left!"

The others take him at his word. He's the expert, and there's no time to argue.

DOZENS OF DRUIDS mill around the archive house, their voices hushed whispers as they speculate about the robbery. Then silence falls as Tanglewood and Faewind walk toward the door, their faces drawn and heads held high.

Tanglewood's voice rings out, firm and resolute. "Everyone except for Leafrunner, go back to your work. Faewind and I will take care of this." Everyone swiftly complies.

The two druids enter the house and scan the shelves. Trembling, Leafrunner approaches the wooden table at the center of the room, where the map to Excalibur lies.

"What happened?" Faewind demands, walking toward him.

"Uh... I came to get..." Leafrunner starts, his voice shaking in fear.

"You don't have to be afraid, Leafrunner. Merlin is powerful, and we know he was here because we felt his magic," Tanglewood reassures him.

"I promise I didn't see him!" the young druid exclaims.

"Start from the beginning," Faewind orders in a soft voice.

Leafrunner inhales slowly before continuing, "I was here to collect a document for school, but as I walked in, I saw three young people! One of them was called Arthur. So, I activated the alarm to warn everyone!"

Tanglewood and Faewind look grave. "What did they take?" Tanglewood asks.

"Nothing! But this plaque was out when it's normally stored over there," Leafrunner responds, pointing to the tray behind him.

The two druids cautiously approach the table as Leafrunner anxiously watches them.

"Very well, you may leave," Faewind tells him.

"We're not going to pursue them?" Leafrunner asks, surprised. "Some men tried catching up to them, but they got away. But it'll be easy for us to track them down with magic!" he says, grinning.

"Don't worry, we will give the instructions," Tanglewood replies abstractedly. "Now go. I need to talk with Faewind."

Leafrunner hurries out of the archive house, thanking his good fortune that he isn't facing any repercussions for what happened on his watch.

As soon as they are alone, Faewind asks Tanglewood, "What do we do? Even if the map is still there, they surely read it! We cannot let them take Excalibur; the fate of England is at stake."

Gazing out the window into the woods, Tanglewood takes a moment to reflect before responding. "You are right. We cannot let them find it. Let's gather the council and head to the cave, where we will wait for them. When they arrive—because believe me, they will—we will strike!"

The two druids hurry from the house and head toward the council room.

CHAPTER 16
THE SAVIORS

L iam and Aria jog along, breathing heavily, but start to slow down as the magnificent oak tree comes into sight again. They are trudging as they enter the clearing.

Liam bends over, hands on his knees, trying to catch his breath. Aria joins him shortly after, opting to stretch instead to release her back pain.

"Geez, it's too bad there's not an obstacle race during Sportapalooza," Liam pants. "Because we're training for it like elite athletes!"

"Are you sure you want to go through that again?" Aria retorts, as red as a tomato.

Arthur and Merlin eventually catch up with them, moving at a slower but steady pace. "You okay?" Liam asks, noting that Merlin and Arthur are much less breathless than he and Aria are.

"Nothing like a little forest run to pep you up!" Arthur responds, beaming. Aria and Liam stare at him, perplexed. How can he be so unaffected by their run when he's always struggled to keep up with them? Not to mention Merlin, who previously nearly had a heart attack just walking.

Seeing the pair's astonished expressions, Merlin pulls a small, empty vial from his robe. "I admit, we gave ourselves a little magical boost!"

"Nice of you to share," Liam responds sarcastically.

"You two are young and trained. You don't need potions to run," Merlin explains, justifying himself.

"We'll save you some next time. Promise!" Arthur adds sincerely.

"N-next time?" Liam stammers. He sincerely hopes the rest of the journey will be smoother, although deep down he strongly doubts it.

"Let's go check out the tree instead of wasting time," Aria suggests before dashing toward it, her batteries already fully recharged.

"I told you she didn't need a potion," Merlin chimes in before following her. Watching him, Liam can't help but roll his eyes. The old man seems to be at least thirty years younger!

Aria is inspecting the crack that rises from the roots to the first branch of the oak tree, her smartphone held up in front of her. Then she looks around the circular clearing and examines the trails that branch off it. "When moon doth glow with argent light, Three stones aligned will guide thee right. Two as twins stand, steadfast and bold, The third in line, a secret it holds," she recites softly before looking up at the sky and then down again at one of the paths.

"Let me read!" Liam demands. Aria silently hands over the phone before running to one of the paths. Merlin regards the device in Liam's hands; he has never seen such a magical object. Arthur stares in confusion as Liam thrusts the phone into his hands. His palms are slightly sweaty as he takes it.

Arthur is shocked by the warmth of the phone against his skin. Panicking, he shuffles it from one hand to the other before dropping it. Astonished, Liam picks it up.

"What were you thinking!" Liam reprimands him as he examines the phone. It was already quite scratched, and the fall doesn't seem to have made things worse. "If you'd broken it, Aria would've gone mad!"

"I'm sorry, but I don't know this magic," Arthur apologizes, his face tense. "I panicked."

Merlin leans over Liam's shoulder to observe the mysterious machine more closely. "Fascinating," he declares. He glances at Liam, then points to the phone with one finger. "Do you mind if I…?"

"Please do, but don't drop it!" Liam warns.

Merlin eagerly grabs the phone. When he feels its warmth, his hands twitch and he jerks his head slightly back. He examines the device from all angles, carefully inspecting every phone feature.

"I've found them!" Aria shouts from some distance away.

Liam and Arthur quickly make their way to her side, leaving Merlin too engrossed in studying the phone to pay attention. He spends some time tapping at the buttons and muttering in awe as the images on the screen change. Eventually, he looks up to ask Liam a question. But to his great surprise, no one is there.

LIAM AND ARTHUR walk the winding track, which is lined with prickly shrubs. "Ouch," Liam exclaims as a bramble gets caught in his hair. Arthur helps release him, and the two set off again just as Aria's voice reaches their ears.

Eventually, they stumble across a path splitting in two directions, with grassy patches on either side. Aria stands in the middle of the field, crouched like a detective at a crime scene. Her gaze is fixed on three long oval stones nestled in the grass. Hearing footsteps, she lifts her head and gives the boys a huge smile.

"Finally! It's about time," she throws at them before pointing. "Here are the stones the verse talks about. And look! On the last one, there's an arrow pointing to the path on the right. This is the clue to the next place," she explains, proud to have solved this puzzle without anyone's help.

While the two boys silently observe her findings, Aria looks behind them and frowns. "Where's Merlin?" she asks.

"He's messing about with your phone!" Liam replies as he bends down to see the arrow. Aria snickers before shouting for the druid so loudly that the two boys cover their ears.

Liam stands up. "It's okay! He was just super

curious; he thinks it's a magical object!" He grins. Aria can't help but laugh, picturing the druid confronted with future technology. Their laughter is abruptly halted as Merlin arrives, his oversized robe catching on the thorns of the bushes around him.

"Here I am," he declares, giving back the phone to Aria. "What a marvelous object! I didn't quite understand everything, but those balls of all colors popping everywhere... One could even get hooked!" he declares, eyes wide open, a frozen smile on his face.

Aria looks at the screen in an attempt to understand what the druid is talking about. Then she realizes that one of her favorite games is open. Liam, completely baffled, leans in to have a look. When he sees the screen, he can't help but let out a gleeful laugh.

"We better hurry. There are footprints going the same way as the stone points," Arthur says. The group starts walking without further ado, hoping the next clue is not too far away. Liam approaches Aria, wondering how she located the pathway on her first go, when there were so many possibilities.

"Admit it, you got lucky!" he whispers.

"Well, if observing is luck to you, then yes!" She smirks.

Liam frowns, trying to understand what Aria said. When she sees that he's not getting it right away, she explains that the full moon was shining over this side of the forest last night, leading her to believe the stones must be there. Impressed but far too proud to admit it, Liam remains silent. A joyful cry from ahead saves him from further awkwardness. Arthur is pointing to two stunning black horses, approaching them down the path.

Merlin's face contorts as he looks at them. He raises his hand in front of Arthur, signaling him to stop. Without a word, he slowly marches toward the horses, his gaze fixed on them.

"What is it, Merlin?" Arthur asks, perplexed.

"Don't you remember what I taught you about druids?" Merlin replies as he glances at each of the horses. "They can transform into any animal." Sharply, he snaps his fingers, but nothing happens. Merlin's face lights up with joy. "It looks like we no longer have to walk!" he exclaims.

"We're lucky they're already harnessed!" Arthur comments. "I wonder why they are here," he adds, rubbing his chin.

"No time to find that out, my boy," Merlin responds hastily. "We need to go quickly!"

"Do you want to go on horseback?" Liam asks,

perplexed. He winces as he looks at the two giant horses coming their way. Large animals make him nervous; their movements are so swift and unpredictable.

"Great idea!" Aria exclaims as she looks at her phone one more time. "The next verse is quite obvious, I think. We need to find a lake," she says as Arthur and Merlin pet the animals. She looks around at the endless trees and bushes. "It may be quite far, so we better go!"

"But wait! We can't steal horses!" Liam exclaims dramatically.

The other three stare at him as if this was nonsense.

"That's not stealing! They must be here to help the persons looking for Excalibur," Aria explains in response to Liam's puzzled expression.

"Liam, ride with Merlin, and Aria, come with me!" Arthur orders while petting one of the horses, who is delighted with this princely treatment. Aria quickly strides toward the horse Arthur is holding, and he helps her mount it. Merlin gracefully climbs atop the second steed and orders it to go closer to Liam. The boy takes a few steps back as the horse approaches, his arms stretching out in defense.

"What's going on?" Merlin asks, surprised.

"He's afraid because he fell off a pony during a riding lesson when we were little," Aria says bluntly, angering Liam.

"You don't have to tell everyone!" he snaps.

"Well, Liam, if you don't confront your fear, you'll never overcome it," Aria lectures him.

"We'll see what you say when you come face to face with a raccoon!" Liam retorts, knowing full well his best friend's phobias.

Growing impatient, Merlin gives the horse a nudge, causing it to advance on Liam without giving him time to react. Merlin catches the boy from the ground with a surprising strength and deposits him on the horse behind him. Liam clutches the old druid around the waist, his heart pounding with fear.

"Not too fast!" he pleads.

Merlin gives the horse a sharp tap, and it takes off rapidly down the pathway, kicking up soil as it races along.

CHAPTER 17
KARMA

Merlin gallops along the narrow trail, tall trees looming above him and nearby bushes catching on his robe. Branches snap, and leaves crunch beneath the powerful hooves of his horse. Eyes full of mischief and determination, he maneuvers the mighty steed with an agility that belies his age. He whips around bulging rocks and leaps over sprawling, contorted roots. Liam clings to the druid's robe, his heart pounding. Every time they miraculously dodge an obstacle, he screws his eyes shut, hoping they survive this treacherous ride in one piece.

Just a few frantic paces behind them, Arthur and Aria race along with their hair wild in the wind. Arthur, his hands steady and assured on the reins, guides their horse with natural ease, a broad smile spread across his face as they gallop along the trail. Aria, her arms securely wrapped around Arthur, laughs fearlessly at every daring leap and swift dodge. Her cheering reverberates through the wood, mingling with the distant hoots of owls and drowning out the gentle rustling of hidden animals.

"Can you stop laughing like that?" Liam shouts, his face dripping with sweat.

"Come on, this is so fun!" Aria retorts with gleaming eyes. "I'm sure you wish I was driving, my dear Liam!" she adds with a grin. So many times, her best friend has attempted to stop her from maneuvering anything due to her *sometimes*-reckless attitude.

Liam's eyes squeeze shut as Merlin barely dodges another gigantic rock on the path. "I never thought I would say that. But yes, I wish you were driving! He's even worse than you. I never thought that could be possi... Ahhhh!" Liam screams as he feels claws clenching in his hair. He shakes his head in every direction to get rid of the animal. The horse is moving so fast that when Liam finally manages to shake off the little animal, it gets propelled backward, to land like a pancake on Arthur's face, all four paws spread star-like, blinding him. Reflexively,

Arthur pulls the reins to signal the horse to stop. His steed halts abruptly, raising its front hooves so high in the air that the two riders' thud to the ground like stones. Aria is squashed under Arthur, who is still blinded by the squirrel wriggling on his face.

"Ouch!" Aria cries out, squashed like a leaf on the ground. But she's still smiling.

Quick, Arthur rolls to the side to free her

"Sorry!" he says as he scoops up the squirrel, which has fallen to the ground.

"No worries, that's the risk of going on an adventure!" she responds cheerfully before standing —but her legs buckle with the pain.

Arthur rises to his feet with much less effort, as Aria had served as a cushion for his fall. "Are you hurt?" he queries.

The squirrel that caused the accident is now nestled in Arthur's hands. He pets its little head.

"I'll be fine," Aria exclaims as she finally manages to straighten her legs. "It's nothing I'm not used to. That's what happens when you love taking risks. You learn to take a few tumbles!" Her eyes twinkle, and she watches curiously as Arthur starts tenderly stroking the squirrel's fur.

Realizing that the hoofbeats of the horse behind them have faded, Merlin pulls back on his horse's reins to get it to slow down and turn. To his utter astonishment, he spots the other horse peacefully grazing on the grass in the distance. Its riders are lying on the ground behind it.

Merlin slaps his horse's flank to spring to their rescue. When he reaches the site of the accident, Arthur is holding one of the most enchanting creatures of the forest in his hand. Merlin's heart warms as he looks at his son, showing affection to the squirrel.

"Ha-ha-ha!" Liam snickers, pointing at his best friend, earning puzzled looks from everyone. "I'm not making fun of you, Arthur; I'm making fun of Aria!" he explains. "She's always fishing out moral lessons, and now karma has hit her. Who'll be afraid to get back on the horse now?"

Without warning, the steed underneath Liam lets out an ear-piercing scream and rears up on its hind legs. Taken by surprise, Liam plops to the ground below, much to the amusement of the others.

Aria moves toward her friend and holds out her hand. "Not me, my dear Liam! By now, you should know that I'm used to performing stunts much more impressive than this one!" Liam grabs her hand, smiling. He must admit that he's been struck by karma this time.

"You win this one!" He grins before glancing at Arthur, who is still petting the squirrel. "The fall must have shaken him up because I've never seen him like this. And that terrifying beast is my attacker!" The animal glares at him. "I'm kidding, I'm kidding!" he quickly adds, making pacifying gestures with his hands amidst the laughter of the others.

"What can I say? You've all rubbed off on me!" Arthur exclaims, winking at them.

"That's all well and good, but we'd better get back in the saddle. Lancelot won't wait for us!" Merlin interjects from atop his horse.

Liam bites his lip as he glances over his shoulder at the path behind Merlin. The journey to the mysterious lake might still be a long one.

"You know what, Liam? Go with Arthur. I'll go with Merlin; he seems to be a fan of strong emotions." Aria beams as she skips toward Merlin, who is more than happy to change passengers. He could barely breathe with Liam behind him. The boy was tugging so vigorously on his robe that it was starting to strangle him!

Liam rushes to join Arthur, who sets the squirrel

free. In a moment, they are all ready to go. Merlin is
the first to give a signal for his horse to set off. The
druid enjoys Aria's happy cries along the journey;
they're drastically different from the moans of his
previous passenger.

LANCELOT HAS BEEN WALKING for what feels like an
eternity, dragging his feet with every step. His eyes
are so weary that his vision blurs. He is determined
not to let his fatigue show. He whispers under his
breath, "A king does not weaken…"

Suddenly, he pauses and takes a second to shut
his eyes before opening them and peering ahead. Far
off in the distance, he sees blue lines resembling
water, surrounded by trees.

Uncertain if he's seeing things, he lifts his hand
to act as a visor, blocking the sun. Yes, he is sure: the
glimmering blue expanse in the distance can only be
a lake. He walks faster, spurred on by the sight of his
goal.

He continues down the grassy, tree-lined path,
and eventually finds himself in a large circular clearing. A lake lies at its center, surrounded by white
pebbles. The sun's rays reflect in the water, creating

a magical blue hue. Rocky hills line one shore, with large pebbles and stones filling the gap between them and the water. The dense forest covers the rest of the landscape.

Liam steps into the tranquil scene, wearing an expression of triumph. The peaceful moment is briefly disrupted by an indistinct noise from the path, but he ignores it, intent on his task.

He steps toward the lake, ready to step into the water. However, the sound from the woods is getting louder and he turns away to check the path. His expression turns tense as he spots two horses galloping in his direction. Though far away, he can distinguish the shapes of two people on each steed.

Fear races through him. Is this group of riders here to take Excalibur? Will they attack him? He's heard the rumors of thieves in the forest. Lancelot no longer has time to think and frantically looks around for a place to hide. Spotting a large tree not far away, he runs and hides behind its trunk just as the horses enter the clearing.

CHAPTER 18
EXCALIBUR

T anglewood and Faewind are the first to exit the council chamber. It has been decided that they, along with two other highly ranked druids from the council, will travel to the cavern where Excalibur is hidden. Hopefully, Lancelot will make it to the stone and be able to free the sword from its rock before anyone else. Merlin's magic set a specific condition that cannot be undone —the person pulling the sword from the rock will become King of England.

The sun glints off the druids' emerald robes as they stride toward the forest. The other villagers watch them with curiosity; not every day do they get to see some of the most powerful magicians in all the land go on a perilous mission.

Faewind glances at Tanglewood and remarks, "We can only hope Lancelot reaches Excalibur first."

Tanglewood remains still for a moment before replying, "Yes, we can hope, but knowing Merlin, I'm not optimistic."

"His magic can't work to find Excalibur. Remember, we cast that spell!" Faewind reminds him.

Their conversation halts as they arrive at the first trees, marking the border between the forest and the village. Tanglewood looks back at his fellow druids before declaring, "Remember, dear companions, Merlin is not to be underestimated. He's a dangerous man with immense power, and he'll do everything possible to see his adopted son take the throne. Let's stay together and keep moving until we reach the cave. Time is of the essence! If we don't get there soon, England could fall," he warns.

Without a word, the group of druids all snap their fingers simultaneously. In a split second, they transform from humans into animals. Some morph into cats, and others become wolves. Immediately, they race through the woods, winding around the trees and veering away from the trail outlined on the map. Their destination: Excalibur's hiding place.

TWO HORSES STAGGER into the lake clearing at high speed. Everyone is instantly mesmerized by the scene. The air is still, except for the occasional birdsong from nearby trees. Sunlight glints off the dark, midnight-blue water and shines brightly on the white rocks beside it. All in all, it is a wonderfully serene scene.

The horses stride toward the water, eager to quench their thirst after the intense ride.

"Wow," Aria exclaims, her eyes sparkling. "This place feels magical!"

Merlin smiles. He often visited places like this before being confined to his bubble.

"It's magnificent!" Arthur chimes in. "I haven't seen anywhere this beautiful since—"

"It's been a long time, my son, I know! But soon, you will be king. You can go anywhere you want!"

Aria and Liam frown; the adventure is far from over. But before they can point this out, Arthur exclaims, "Merlin, we still have to find Excalibur!"

"*And* you have to pull it from the stone!" Liam insists, but his expression softens when Arthur glances at him. "Don't get me wrong—I understand it's difficult."

Arthur replies, "You're absolutely right!"

Aria bends over to study the ground.

"What are you doing now?" Liam asks.

"I'm just checking. There are…" Aria loses her balance and plants face-first onto the grassy ground. "Footprints," she manages to say.

Liam and Arthur exchange amused glances as Merlin slides off his horse to help her up. "Well, my girl, you certainly have a knack for ending up sprawled on the ground!"

"It's true," Liam mutters under his breath, causing Arthur to laugh even more.

Aria gives a mocking smirk before heading onward, her eyes focused on the ground. She stops as she notices the footprints leading into the forest, thinking they don't make sense. She pulls out her phone and scans the screen. "In a cavern deep, where shadows play, a test of balance shall lead the way. Sacrifice, not the life that blooms, And Excalibur's rest will flee the glooms," she recites before surveying her surroundings.

The words from the last riddle force Arthur and Liam to refocus. They jump off the horse and join Aria in her quest for the hidden cave. They begin to scrutinize every nook and cranny of the clearing, though the blinding sunlight makes the task a challenge.

"There's too much sun. I can't see anything!" Liam exclaims, his eyes stinging from all the reflections.

Merlin turns to his companion, grinning broadly. "Easily fixed!" he cries before quickly snapping his fingers. Out of thin air, clouds form and obscure the bright sky, dimming its brightness just enough that they can see without dazzling their eyes.

Suddenly, Aria begins to hop on the spot, her breath quickening with excitement. "Look there!" she and Liam yell simultaneously, pointing at one of the rocky hillocks.

At the bottom of the hillock is a small, semicircular opening partially blocked by some large stones. Suddenly, Merlin starts running around the lake. "We must make haste," he says. "There's no time to waste!"

The others are astonished to see the old druid attempt to run, almost tripping on his robe with each step. They follow him, soon reaching the edge of the grass and pebbles. There, they overtake him and start to skip from rock to rock in the direction of the cave, no one saying a word as they concentrate on the task at hand. Suddenly, Aria halts abruptly and turns around. Liam, standing just behind her, nearly falls.

"Aria!" he shouts, his voice full of surprise. He reaches out with his other hand and grabs onto a nearby rock just in time to keep his balance.

"Excuse me, did you hear that?" Aria's voice is distant as she stares at a patch of grass right by the shore. Liam turns to look behind them but only sees Merlin advancing at a snail's pace. "It's just Merlin. We should keep moving before something happens," he says. Aria turns and resumes hopping from one stone to another, barely touching the ground before leaping again.

But Arthur is the first to arrive at the cave entrance, his days of playing hopscotch on boulders in the clearing paying off.

Aria and Liam hurry to catch up as he vanishes inside the cave. When they reach him, they cry out in amazement. A granite terrace serves as a vestibule leading into the space beyond. Inside lies a small tranquil, azure lake illuminated by shimmering stones set into the ceiling of rock overhead. Arthur strides toward it, his eyes lighting up with wonder as he takes in the sight.

"Do you think Excalibur is beyond the water?" Liam asks, awestruck.

"We need to go check," Aria responds, moving up next to Arthur. "Let's just hope you can swim," she says grumpily.

"Swim? What a strange idea!" Merlin's voice booms out, shocking them as he emerges from nowhere. Merlin raises both hands and makes a sharp movement in the air. The cave begins to tremble so violently that Aria grabs Arthur's cloak, and he has to lurch around to keep his balance. Liam's arms whirl like windmills to keep himself upright.

Long flat stones rise from the water and form a bridge. Then the shaking stops as abruptly as it had begun. "Swim! What an odd idea!" Merlin mutters as he strides toward the water and onto the stepping stones. After reaching the other side, he turns around and addresses them. "Don't just stand there like statues! Excalibur is calling us!" he exclaims, throwing both arms in the air.

One by one, they dash onto the magical bridge. As they reach the other side, Merlin guides them into an adjacent room, dimly lit by sparkling crystals set in its roof and a few torches hung on the rocky walls of the cave. In the center, atop a stone podium, sits a large, faceted rock with the sword Excalibur embedded in its heart.

LANCELOT SNEAKS ALONG THE PATH, careful not to be seen. The girl nearly spotted him, but his reflexes kicked in, and he immediately dropped to the ground, the tall grass covering him. They must be on the same quest as him. What else would bring them here, past the trees and toward a cave, if not to hunt for Excalibur? With his disheveled beard and green cloak, the old man is obviously a druid. Maybe it's Merlin who betrayed the famous Circle of Druids? Everyone in England knows him! And the two horses the group came with are the same ones he met at the beginning of the path. Lancelot tries not to think about how much time he could have saved if he had accepted their offer of a ride.

Lancelot slowly makes his way toward the rocky path bordering the hillocks. The only person visible is the old druid, and he appears to be quite scared of falling as he keeps his gaze focused on the ground. Taking no chances, Lancelot stays pressed close to the cliff, his outfit blending perfectly with the rocks.

Lancelot is swift and manages to reach the cave entrance shortly after the old man enters. He takes cover behind a rocky outcrop, suppressing his breathing so he can try to hear what's going on inside. Muffled voices echo out of the cave, but the words are too garbled for him to make out.

Lancelot waits until the echoes of voices in the cave dissipate. Then, he peeks around the cave, admiring the rocky formations. Suddenly, a cry from the other side grabs his attention. Without hesitation, he half-leaps, half-flies over the stones leading him to the other bank.

CHAPTER 19
EXCALIBUR

The rock where Excalibur sits glows in the light emanating from its podium. Its gold handle is covered with sparkling precious stones and diamonds. Its silver blade reflects the light even more. Here, in the middle of this enchanting cave, rests the fate of England.

The children are awestruck, staring at Excalibur as it radiates mysterious power. Merlin stands back, keeping his gaze fixed on the sword he thrust into this rock many years ago. He hasn't seen it since he cast the spell. The sword elicits a flood of emotion in him, and he can't help but shed tears.

"It's…" Aria pauses, her voice trailing off as she gingerly steps toward the sword, almost reluctant to approach it.

"Magnificent!" Liam says. After a moment of silence, he turns to Arthur, gesturing for him to go. "It's all yours," he adds. But Arthur stands frozen, his face displaying the turmoil of emotions within him. "Go on, or else I will!" Liam adds with a teasing smile, defusing the tension.

"Maybe that's the solution," Arthur finally replies, winking at him. His gaze shifts downward to the sword as his legs stiffen and his knuckles clench around its hilt. He raises his head, examining each of them.

His voice is serious as he tells Aria and Liam, "You should remove Excalibur. I never would have found it without you—and I would have stayed stubborn and..."

"Spoiled rotten?" Liam interjects with a sly smile.

"Indeed!" Arthur replies, smiling back. Merlin's expression is one of utter confusion as he listens.

Aria moves forward, pointing out, "You were the one who chose to change yourself. We just gave you a nudge in the right direction. The sword is yours now. Besides, Liam and I don't live here. We have to return home, and England needs a king! And I thought it was your biggest dream?"

Arthur pauses for a moment before replying, "It is my biggest dream, but I want to deserve it.

Liam grins. "Come on, Arthur, you deserve it! And Aria is right. Our adventure was great, but there's no place like Sommetville!" The three children giggle.

"Go on, my boy, before Lancelot gets here," Merlin urges him, trembling.

After a fleeting glance at his friends, Arthur advances solemnly toward the podium. The suspense is palpable as he finally marches to his long-awaited destiny.

But just as Arthur is about to reach the podium, two cats appear from a nook and jump out in front of him, changing into humans in mid-air. Arthur leaps back, petrified. Before he can do anything else, three other animals pop out of the nook and also turn into humans, forming a ring around the sword.

Without wasting a moment, Merlin confidently strides to Arthur's side and addresses the two persons before him. "Greetings, Tanglewood and Faewind," he declares loudly, unbothered by their menacing glares.

Lancelot has found a marvelous spot from which to observe the events unfolding before him. Upon seeing Excalibur, he has to rub his eyes several times; the sword is even more beautiful than he imagined.

Quickly analyzing the situation, he decides to launch a surprise attack from the rear, with his dagger primed and ready. However, just before he can leap toward Excalibur, he stands in awe as he sees the animals surrounding them transform into humans. The sight is so astonishing that he nearly falls backward.

He is certain this is the Circle of Druids. Reining in his impatience—hopefully, they will deal with Merlin and give Lancelot a clear run at the rock—he waits to see the situation unfold.

"Hello, Merlin," Faewind responds, her voice deep. "We are here…"

"To prevent Arthur from fulfilling his destiny, I see that. I see you brought Daelan and Sylva with you as well," Merlin interjects, glancing at the two other druids.

"Do not play the innocent, Merlin; you know

very well that Arthur's destiny has changed. And you only have yourself to blame!" Tanglewood retorts.

"We trusted you, and you played us, Merlin," Daelan says, defying him with his gaze.

Aria glances at Liam, who is too focused on the confrontation to notice. If they want Arthur to take Excalibur, they need to move swiftly.

She scans the area: Tanglewood and Faewind are standing in front of them, and the other two druids are on each side. Together, they form a semi-circle around the rock. She and Liam can immobilize Tanglewood and Faewind, leaving a path for Arthur to dash toward the rock and seize Excalibur. If they move fast enough, the druids on either side of the sword won't have time to react.

She finally catches Liam's attention and begins to sign out the plan with her hands. After several reiterations, Liam finally understands and nods his head.

"Arthur's destiny has not changed! It's you who have turned against me because of nonsensical prophecies!" Merlin's voice grows louder, fueled by the bitterness he has harbored for years.

Sylva steps forward. "What prophecies are you talking about?" she asks, perplexed.

Suddenly, Aria gives Liam a wink. Without a

word, they spring into action, Liam tackling Tangle-wood while Aria goes for Faewind. "Arthur! Grab it now!" Liam yells, clinging onto Tanglewood, who stumbles backward, taken by surprise.

Without hesitating, Arthur lunges for Excalibur. Daelan and Sylva sprint toward him, only to be halted mid-step. A wave of Merlin's hand flings them to opposite ends of the cave.

Just as Arthur nears the podium, Faewind pushes Aria away and morphs into a cat. The feline leaps at Arthur, its claws snagging his cloak. Arthur squirms and shuffles, trying to shake her off, but Faewind climbs onto his head, obscuring his vision.

As Liam struggles on Tanglewood's back, the druid abruptly goes still. With a snap of the fingers, he flings Liam toward Merlin. The old wizard readies a spell, but Tanglewood is quicker. With a swift motion, he cloaks Excalibur in a shimmering shield.

Aria scrambles to her feet, dashing to Arthur's aid. But before she can reach him, Daelan captures her in a tight grip. Spotting Aria in trouble, Liam pushes through his pain from his fall and runs toward Arthur. Tanglewood tries to intervene, but Merlin's spell forms a barrier around Liam, repelling all magical advances. However, Sylva erupts from behind and holds him tight around the chest.

Arthur gives his head a fierce shake, dislodging Faewind. Gasping for breath, he makes another run for the podium. But Tanglewood's magic sends him soaring backward to land near Merlin. Faewind, now back in her human form, stands proudly by Tanglewood. Together they form a guard for Excalibur.

"We will not let you ruin England!" Tanglewood shouts, his expression hard.

"You cannot do this!" Merlin shouts back. "I am the one who cast a spell on Excalibur, and the rule is simple: whoever finds it and removes it will be crowned king!"

"You cast this spell without consulting the Circle of Druids. You had no right! And now, with the protective shield I just created, only the person most fit to rule will be able to pierce it," Tanglewood declares, then smiles tightly.

"I can see you remember some of the magic tricks I taught you, Tanglewood. But where is your Lancelot, anyway? I suppose he could not decipher a simple riddle!" Merlin declares sarcastically.

The conversation is cut short by the sudden appearance of a young man. Lancelot moves silently into the cave and sees the astonished faces of those gathered around Excalibur. "I am here. My apologies for being tardy!" He smiles as he marches over to stand beside Faewind.

Liam struggles to break free, but Sylva's grip on him tightens so much he can barely breathe.

Merlin grimaces. "And you really think that your Lancelot has the qualities required to rule the country?" he replies.

"Lancelot will be the best king England has ever known!" declares Faewind, her voice brimming with confidence.

Aria's soft cough turns all eyes her way. "Actually, that's not true." Her unexpected certainty takes Tanglewood and Faewind aback.

Tanglewood raises an eyebrow. "Who are you, anyway?"

Before Aria can reply, Merlin chimes in, grinning cheekily, "The person who is going to prove you wrong!"

Aria contradicts him. "I can't *prove* you wrong as I don't have my history books. But I can guarantee you that Lancelot will not become the best king England has ever known."

Uncertainty and annoyance flicker in Tanglewood and Faewind's eyes. Lancelot, ready to speak up in his own defense, is silenced by a quick gesture from Faewind.

"And you think we will just believe a young girl without proof? We don't even know who you are!" Faewind responds haughtily.

Aria rolls her eyes, "I *am* sorry. Where are my manners? I am Aria, and over there is my best friend Liam. We're from Sommetville," she exclaims proudly, "and we have a minor habit of traveling through history to save the day!"

"Minor?" Liam retorts, frowning.

"Anyway, as we are from the future, we can guarantee that Lancelot will not be a king to celebrate," Aria continues. "You will even lose your country because of this choice!"

"This is nonsense! I am the greatest knight in England!" Lancelot protests.

"But I am destined to become king!" Arthur retorts gravely, his eyes riveted on his rival.

"I don't even know you!" Lancelot fights back.

Faewind raises her arms, signaling for quiet. A hushed stillness blankets the cave, every breath thick with tension.

Tanglewood's face shows a flicker of doubt as he studies Aria intently. Could they have gotten it wrong? Merlin steps closer, and his two old friends instinctively pull back.

"With all due respect," Merlin begins in a steady voice, "Arthur is destined to be king. And thanks to our time-traveling friends here, we know the unfortunate fate of England under King Lancelot."

Tanglewood's eyes switch to gaze at Merlin. But he maintains a telling silence.

"Tanglewood, I am sure they are lying!" Faewind murmurs. "We hold the fate of England in our hands. We must not fail."

"Why would we make this up?" Liam interjects, drawing all eyes to him. "Seriously, we've got nothing to gain from lying!"

Faewind raises an eyebrow. "Let me guess, Merlin brought you here and won't let you go until you complete your task? That sounds like a good reason to lie. And knowing Merlin as I do, he's probably spun you quite the tale."

"I've spoken only the truth!" Merlin responds, his voice filled with authority.

"And I suppose you didn't paint us as the villains?" Tanglewood finally chimes in.

"You tried everything to eliminate us, to put your Lancelot on the throne and deny Arthur his rightful inheritance!" Merlin shouts, his voice trembling with years of suppressed rage.

"Do not talk nonsense, Merlin. We have never tried to eliminate you. It's against our law, and you know it," Tanglewood counters, raising his arms in exasperation.

"Lancelot should be king," Faewind insists, "you know that too. Don't be hard-headed, Merlin! No doubt these children are liars like you!"

Aria and Liam's faces cloud with anger. "You have some nerve"—Liam's voice rises with indignation—"calling us liars when you can't even admit what you've done to Merlin! I'd never treat my best friend the way you did!"

For a brief moment, Sylva's hold loosens. Liam shoves with all his might, breaking free. Aria follows suit, pushing off Daelan. In no time, the pair are sprinting toward Merlin.

With a swift gesture, Merlin transforms Daelan and Sylva into rabbits. Tanglewood and Faewind stand rooted in place, caught off guard by the whirlwind of events. As Faewind begins to muster a spell, Merlin intervenes. "Don't even think about it, Faewind. You know I'm the more powerful magician here."

"Merlin," Tanglewood interjects in a gentle but

firm tone, "I have no idea what you told these children, but you know we wanted to see Arthur become king. If only you had respected our druidic golden rule."

Merlin stays quiet, his eyes fixed on Tanglewood. Aria gasps in surprise as realization dawns, the pieces of the puzzle suddenly clicking together.

CHAPTER 20
THE DRUIDS' SECRET

L iam glances at Aria, noting her familiar 'aha!' expression. "What is it?" he inquires, cutting through the tense hush.

Aria slaps her forehead, looking incredulous. "How did I miss this?" she murmurs, then pivots excitedly toward Liam. "Do you remember our lesson on Lancelot? How the druids placed him on the throne?"

"Yes, I already told you," Liam replies. "Lancelot grabs Excalibur, and shortly after that, invaders storm England." Faewind and Tanglewood exchange shocked glances at this revelation.

"But think about the druids!" Aria prods. "Remember their golden rule?" Her eyes are twinkling.

Liam scrunches his face in thought. "Um… how about you just tell me? It's like a pressure cooker up here!" He points to his head.

Aria gives an exaggerated sigh. "Liam, one day you'll need to learn our entire history lessons, not just the fun parts."

"Why would I want to deprive you of the joy of teaching me something?" he retorts playfully. The druids shift their gaze between the two adventurers, trying to puzzle out their conversation.

Aria beams. "True," she agrees and takes a deep breath before saying, "Why did the druids manage the choice of the future King of England? Well, druids are the keepers of wisdom and knowledge. They must ensure that the king embodies balance and unity, connecting all creatures, safeguarding nature, and championing peace." As she concludes, Tanglewood and Faewind nod in affirmation while Merlin's gaze drops to the ground.

Liam greets Aria's words with a blank expression. Then the realization hits him like a ton of bricks. "So, that's why they don't want Arthur as king!" he gasps, swiftly turning to Merlin. "You lied to us!"

Merlin remains stoic, a statue under the weight of the revelation.

Arthur jolts in surprise, his face twisting in confusion. "What do you mean?" he demands.

Aria starts to explain. "You said you were only placed inside this magical bubble at age ten, correct?" Arthur nods. "But Merlin told us the Circle of Druids rejected you as king as soon as you were born, due to a prophecy."

"It wasn't true! They reconsidered when they saw how you became," Liam interjects.

Merlin stands frozen as Arthur's eyes find him. They are filled with questions.

"You were no longer fit to become king because you lacked the virtues the Druid Circle lives by: bravery, honesty, compassion, and kindness," Aria explains, sounding proud of putting the pieces together.

Amused, Tanglewood remarks, "Well, it seems we've got two sharp minds here." His eyes slide over to Merlin, challenging him. "Perhaps it's time to come clean?"

Merlin's expression fluctuates between fury and regret.

"Is what they are saying true, Merlin?" Arthur asks him in a trembling voice.

After a moment of silence, Merlin finally capitulates. "Yes," he says solemnly, "it is true."

MERLIN LOOKS deep into Arthur's eyes. His own are brimming with tears as he takes his son's hands. "I'm sorry, my boy, for lying to you… for everything." He starts sobbing. "When I took you as my son, I was sure I could guide you to become a responsible and just king for this nation. But soon, it all became too much for me. I realized I couldn't make up for your parents' absence by myself, so I was willing to give you anything you wanted without expectation, hoping it would make you feel better. I wanted to give you the confidence you need, so I kept telling you about your destiny so you could realize that your parents' absence didn't mean you were not enough, not valuable."

"Maybe just a smidge too much confidence…" Arthur mumbles into his beard.

"I know now that it was wrong. But it was so hard to see you doubt yourself!" Merlin resumes, more tears welling in his eyes. "I'd made a deal with the Circle of Druids: they'd accept my proposal if I raised you with values that were in harmony with our beliefs. If I failed, someone else would have to replace you. When I noticed my mistake, it was too late to fix it. You were already grown, and I knew there was no going back, so I did all I could to hide the truth from the Circle of Druids," he continues. Arthur, meanwhile, is seeing his childhood scrolling before his eyes.

"But that didn't work," Tanglewood interjects in a compassionate voice, moving closer to Merlin.

"Exactly. You are too strong for that," Merlin resumes with a lopsided smile. "The last time I met the council, they had already realized what was happening. They told me you could not become king, but I refused to bend. Eventually, I had to shut you away from the world to safeguard you, creating a bubble so they couldn't find us. When your father passed away, I had to devise a plan. That's when I heard of two adventurers who can move through time and assist people in achieving their destinies and altering the course of history!"

"That's us!" Aria declares, pointing at herself.

"I thought it was the right decision, and I can tell it made much more of a difference than I anticipated. I'm so proud to see you turn into the man I always wanted you to be!" Merlin's voice quivers as he hides his face in his hands. Arthur hugs him while everyone looks on, touched by the moment.

Except for Lancelot, who shrugs his shoulders, unmoved. Then, a thought flashes into his mind. While all eyes are on Merlin, the path to Excalibur is clear. He has no more time for waiting; he must act. When he holds the sword, England's throne will be his.

Without hesitation, Lancelot sprints toward the stone. As he jumps onto the platform, he is swiftly pushed back by an invisible wall. "Ouch!" he yells, falling hard on the cave floor.

Everyone gasps, seeing Lancelot on the ground while the shimmering shield is still intact around the stone. Tanglewood and Faewind share a worried look. Has destiny taken another path?

Merlin, smiling now, steps forward. "See? If Lancelot was really meant to be king, he would've gotten past your magic bubble. You made that wall, didn't you?" he asks Tanglewood.

"But that doesn't mean Arthur can do it," Faewind quickly says.

"Arthur. Your turn to try," Tanglewood demands authoritatively, surprising everyone.

"Who? Me?" Arthur stammers, not having anticipated this twist.

"No, your twin!" the Druid responds sarcastically. The remark brings a flurry of laughter from Aria and Liam. Druids are funnier than they let on!

Everyone parts and forms an aisle as legs trembling, Arthur strides toward the podium.

CHAPTER 21

THE KING OF ENGLAND

When Arthur reaches the platform, he reaches out with a nervous hand. The moment his fingers touch the shimmering shield, it sparkles and vanishes. Everyone in the cave gasps in surprise, their hearts pounding.

Now, nothing lies between Arthur and the sword. He feels a tingle as he grips Excalibur's hilt. After a quick, deep breath, he pulls the sword out easily, and Merlin, Aria, and Liam start cheering loudly.

Faewind stands astonished as she sees the young boy with the sword in his hand. "I can't believe..." she mumbles.

"This is a lesson for us, Faewind," Tanglewood says. "We should never believe that no one can change, however impossible it seems to be." He smiles a little reluctantly.

"My boy!" Merlin exclaims before running toward his adoptive son. Unexpectedly, he hugs Arthur, catching him off guard and nearly causing him to cut himself with the blade. After a breath-stealing embrace, Merlin releases him and kneels before him, bowing his head. "My king!"

Tanglewood and Faewind quickly do the same. Aria and Liam look at each other, puzzled, before deciding to copy them. Arthur feels a wave of emotion when he realizes what's happening. As a child, he longed for this destiny, but it now looks nothing like he had pictured it.

Lancelot is crestfallen. Eventually, he lifts himself off the ground and walks out of the cave without a word, unaware that he will one day be a knight of King Arthur's Round Table. Aria and Liam stand up and follow the others as they go to congratulate the new King of England.

"Well played! We can't wait to see what you do during your reign," Liam declares as he reaches the young monarch.

"My gratitude to you both will never end," Arthur says before hugging them tightly.

Tanglewood and Faewind reach out for Merlin's hand, and the three of them come together.

"You have shown us that change is possible, Merlin," Tanglewood says.

Faewind grins as she tells her childhood friend, "I am sorry, Merlin, for having been hard on you."

"It's alright, I forgive you…" Merlin mumbles.

Faewind laughs. "You did lie to us, so I suppose we are even," she says as Merlin grins at her. "Will you return to the village with us?"

Merlin tilts his head in contemplation before raising his index finger and answering, "On one condition: that I can move my house into the village!"

The other two druids burst into laughter. Their friend certainly hasn't changed!

"Did you know I've discovered a new form of magic?" Merlin keeps talking as he guides them toward the exit, followed by two rabbits. "Colored balls that move everywhere. Fascinating!"

"One other thing—maybe you could switch them back?" Tanglewood asks Merlin, nodding toward the two cats.

"Sorry, I forgot about that!" Merlin apologizes before clapping his hands, reverting Daelan and Sylva instantly to their human forms.

Aria and Liam giggle as they watch. Then Liam exclaims with a grin, "Alright, it's time for us to head back, my dear Aria! We have a tournament to win,"

"You're so right, my dear Liam! But before that, I'd like to…" Aria starts to say, and then disappears with a snap of Merlin's fingers.

"…VISIT…" Aria finishes.

They are sitting on the Sommetville Junior High School field, leaning back on their hands, the frisbee lying between them. The arena is filled with the sound of cheers, as if they'd never left. The sight of Amelia sprinting toward them brings them to their senses. Liam dives for the frisbee while Aria runs toward the field. Liam throws it, and Aria swiftly catches it before Amelia can intercept. The game becomes more and more intense as the teams pass the frisbee to one another, and neither side is able to gain an advantage. Mr. Thornton's whistle blows, signaling the end of play.

John congratulates them, offering his hand for a shake. "Well played! You guys really turned it around."

"I'm just glad we drew!" Amelia chimes in

happily, aware that Aria and Liam usually come out of these games on top.

Liam smirks, warning them not to get too confident. "We still have two competitions left!"

"Come on, you four! Move it!" Mr. Thornton urges. "You have to move to the BranchBounce-Flyers fields," he yells in their direction. Grins spread across the adventurers' faces; they've been practicing for this, under the harshest conditions.

Aria rubs her hands together. "Let's do this. You'll find out just how good Liam and I really are!" she says with a hint of arrogance as she sprints away.

"Unlike you, we've been training!" John teases as he races after her.

"Don't be too sure of yourself," Liam chimes in, excited for the challenge ahead. "We've been putting in a lot of practice lately!"

All four of them sprint toward the next competition, determined to take home the trophy from Sommetville Junior High School's most popular sports event.

Dear Young Dreamers,

I, Merlin, the enigmatic druid from the Arthurian legend, extend to you a greeting as magical as the tales that have carried my name through the corridors of time.

In your adventures, you have journeyed with me, Merlin, through enchanting tales of chivalry, magic, and the legendary King Arthur. However, it is crucial for you, as seekers of truth and knowledge, to discern the line between what history whispers and what legends sing.

Let us first turn the pages to the lessons life imparts. Remember that while it is beautiful to believe in great things, these wonders do not manifest by mere wishful thinking. The universe grants no entitlements; it is through diligence, perseverance, and the sweat of our brows that dreams become reality. As you chase your aspirations, let your actions be your magic, your determination your spell.

King Arthur and I reside as figures covered in mystery in the books of history and myth. King Arthur, greeted as the once and future king, is a character many legends revolve around. Historians and scholars debate his existence, with some tracing his origins to a Briton leader who fought against Saxon invaders. Yet, much of what is known about Arthur comes not from historical records but from medieval romances and folklore.

As for me, Merlin, I am a creation of these very legends. A wizard of profound wisdom, a mentor to Arthur, and a figure intertwined with the mystical elements of these stories. While there is no concrete historical evidence of my existence, the character of Merlin is believed to have been inspired by earlier figures in Welsh folklore, possibly including a bard and a prophet.

These stories, filled with knights, chivalry, and magical adventures, belong more to the realm of legend than historical fact. The Round Table, Excalibur, Camelot, and the Quest for the Holy Grail are all elements of a rich narrative that has evolved over centuries, captivating the hearts and imaginations of people across the world.

As you journey through life, let the tales of Arthur and I, Merlin, remind you that while not all stories are true in the historical sense, their essence can guide you toward living a life filled with purpose, courage, and wisdom. Strive to be like the noble knights: valiant in your pursuits and true to your heart. And remember, in each of you lies the potential to write your own legend, one that future generations will look to for inspiration and guidance.

With magical blessings and timeless wisdom,
Merlin

Dear fellow adventurers,

Wowza! We're bursting with excitement as we scribble these words to thank you for joining us on one of the most incredible, action-packed adventure of our lives!

Before we wrap up this wild ride, we want to shout a big THANK YOU to you, our fearless comrades. Your support, energy, and pure awesomeness have made this adventure one for the record books.

Now, as you close this book and head back to your everyday lives, remember to keep that adventurous spark alive. Let curiosity be your compass, keep exploring, and let your imaginations run wild! The world is a playground of endless wonders waiting just for YOU.

So, until we meet again, may your days be filled with endless laughter, wild adventures, and the most epic tales ever told!

Happy exploring, you amazing adventurers!

Cheers!

Aria   Liam

CHECK OUT ALL THE

ADVENTURES

WE'VE BEEN IN

A thrilling Egyptian adventure.

Save Caesar and face Rome's hidden challenges.

Navigate Atlantis's secrets to break a powerful curse.

Race against time to save the Incas.

Spooky thrills in Dracula's realm.

An adventure into Santa's realm to save Christmas.

ACKNOWLEDGMENTS

Thank you to Anna Bowles, my editor, for her guidance and enthusiasm throughout this new adventure. A special thanks to Stella Marvin, whose insights as a beta reader were invaluable, and Michele from Two Birds Author Service for their meticulous proofreading. Lastly, I'm grateful to Draftss for their exceptional illustrations that truly brought this adventure to life.

ABOUT THE AUTHOR

Coline Monsarrat is a history enthusiast driven by a feverish passion for the captivating and unforgettable stories that unfold within its pages. In her series, *Aria & Liam*, she merges humor and adventure, presenting the colorful escapades of a clumsy duo navigating history and its legends. Through their journey, young readers uncover history's lessons amidst fun-filled adventures.

facebook.com/ColineMonsarratAuthor

instagram.com/colinemonsarrat